FAKE IT UNTIL YOU MAKE IT SEASON 2

A BIMBO TRANSFORMATION NOVEL

SADIE THATCHER

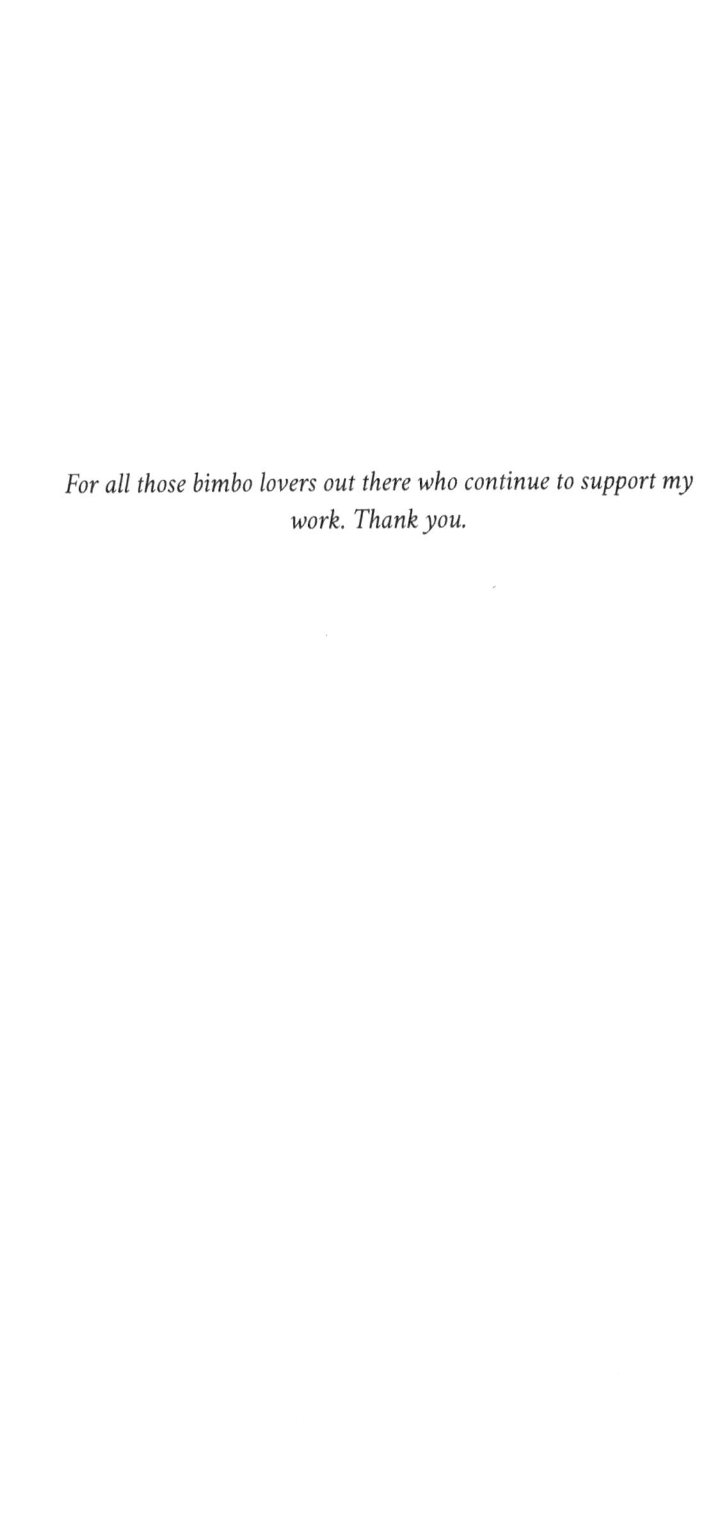

For all those bimbo lovers out there who continue to support my work. Thank you.

CONTENTS

INTRODUCTION

This book is the second "season" of an ongoing serialized story. The story began on my now defunct Patreon and now lives on other serialized platforms. However, the current serialized platform is only available to US readers. For the first time, the broader story of Fake It Until You Make It is available to a worldwide audience in ebook and paperback versions.

Thank you for reading, I hope you enjoy it, and be sure to check out the rest of Fake It Until You Make It story, either in book form when it becomes available, or through a serialized platform.

This season picks up where the previous season left off. The chapter numbers follow the same pattern as the individual episodes in the serialized form. Thus the first chapter or episode in this book begins with chapter 22.

TRADING OFF

It took time for Jessi to recover from getting fucked by her roommate. Candi had been a perfect partner, giving her exactly what she needed. Luckily, Candi was very understanding.

"I've been there before," Candi said sympathetically. "This lifestyle takes stamina."

Jessi knew it was true. There was so much effort she had to put into everything to make sure she was always fuckable. It was hard work, but the rewards were great. Jessi could barely believe how much she had changed and she fully intended to continue her personal transformation.

It was late in the afternoon when Candi suggested they make a visit to the gym for a workout. That had been one of Jessi's strengths beginning during the summer and it was important to her that she continue. Therefore, despite her body still wanting to lounge around after getting fucked by her roommate, she jumped at the opportunity to sweat.

This time, however, rather than Candi showing Jessi how to do things, it was Jessi who had the upper hand. Jessi had spent her summer getting fit and she felt much more confident in the gym than her roommate. Candi had been blessed with a natural figure that required little upkeep, but even she knew the importance of fitness.

Both women dressed as skimpily as they could, wearing sports bras and spandex shorts. Their bodies were on complete display and they reveled in the looks they got from the various men they encountered, both on their way across campus to the fitness center and the men who were already working out. The only significant change that Jessi made was she removed the dangling belly-button piercing that she had borrowed from Candi and replaced it with a simple pink barbell. She did not want it to get caught on anything.

The eyes of the desk clerk who checked students into the fitness center bulged at the sight of Jessi and Candi. Technically the rules forbid bare midriffs, but there was no way the clerk or any of the other student staff were going to tell off the two popular girls. Candi looked natural as the pair moved around the gym, but Jessi still felt a little bit of unease. That was ridiculous compared to what she had done since arriving at school, but she felt it nonetheless.

"I think I need to go shopping again," Jessi said as the pair started on the elliptical machines for a warm up. They were able to workout side by side and continue chatting about whatever popped into their heads. "I don't have enough clothes to keep dressing like I have been."

That was the truth. She had already been shopping for new stuff, but Jessi was wearing several different outfits per day and she could not go repeating them constantly. And she could only borrow clothes from Candi for so long. Besides, there were lots of cute clothes of Candi's that Jessi could not wear due to the differences in their sizes. Candi had big boobs and Jessi did not. That proved to be a significant difference.

"How about tomorrow afternoon?" Candi offered, excited

at the prospect of a trip to the mall. She was always interested in shopping. And having Jessi along would make it all the better. As much fun as it was shopping for herself, she enjoyed shopping for Jessi even more.

Jessi had to think about it for a moment, not wanting a shopping excursion to conflict with anything else on her schedule. However, she realized she had the afternoon free. Jessi had considered arranging for a repeat of Saturday night with Travis, but she could do that anytime. Jessi figured she could even call him tonight if she really wanted to, although she had to admit that getting fucked twice in the same day was plenty. She did not need to add sucking cock to the list of accomplishments for the day. Besides, she had already spent time practicing and figured her throat could use a rest.

After a warm up on the elliptical machine, the pair hit the weights. They both knew that lifting was not going to bulk them up, but it would help make them strong and lean. And that was the kind of results they were going for. It was no fun to just be a weak doll. It was far better to become an active participant in their trysts, even adding a bit of acrobatics if needed to spice things up.

Not that Jessi had a particular plan about what acrobatics to include in her sex life. She was still learning about all of that. However, the idea that she could wrap her legs around a man as he fucked her and actually hold him close was something she wanted to be able to do. Getting fucked against the wall placed the idea in her mind. Yes, she had been able to wrap her legs around the guy as he fucked her, but she had not been strong enough to hold him tight inside her if she wanted to.

Then again, such ideas might have just been part of a pipe dream. Either way, Jessi was excited about what her future entailed. Thatcher College had so many hot guys and she had made herself one of the elite girls who could always be counted on for a good time.

After spending at least half an hour lifting weights, Jessi led Candi through a series of core exercises, activities that just required their body weight to perform. Technically they could have performed these exercises in their dorm room, but it was much more fun gathering the collective gaze of the other gym users. There were several regular gym rats, men who spent more time than was probably necessary developing their upper body muscles. Those men seemed to pay particularly close attention to the two sluts as they worked together on a mat in the corner.

However, it was when Jessi and Candi transitioned to a combination of stretching and yoga that the stares really intensified. It was not so much that they were contorting their bodies in strange positions, because they were not really doing that. Instead, it was the fact they were already showing so much skin and now they were giving anyone who wanted a glimpse of a camel toe or the way their shorts hugged their asses a view that was hard to resist. Even women were staring.

"Hello there, I'm Joe," said one of the obvious regular lifters as Jessi and Candi finished their routine. "I just wanted to compliment the both of you on your complete workout."

Jessi and Candi both smiled, seeing the obvious attractive qualities of their admirer. And it did not hurt that he had waited until they had finished their workout. And it was not like he had just arrived. He had actually already been there before they got to the gym. But he understood the importance of not interrupting people when they were in the middle of their workouts. Jessi and Candi had acted seriously and they got respect for their actions.

"Hi," Jessi said automatically. "I'm Jessi and this is Candi."

"Hi, Joe," Candi said. She reached out and ran her hand along his forearm, tracing the lines of his muscles.

Jessi saw right away her roommate's interest in Joe. After providing so much help, Jessi figured it was about time she returned the favor.

"If you want him, he's yours," Jessi whispered in Candi's ear.

There was an almost imperceptible nod, but there was enough movement for Jessi to pick up on the signal.

"I've got to get back to our room," Jessi said. "But it looks like the two of you have a little catching up to do. See you later, Candi. Nice to meet you, Joe."

Joe and Candi both waved to Jessi, but their eyes never left each other. They were both infatuated with each other. Had Jessi not already gotten plenty of fucking in that day, she would have considered fighting Candi for a chance with Joe. He was hot, although in a musclebound sort of way. He definitely was no Cole. But it was only fair that the roommates share. Besides, there was a high probability that Jessi would have her own shot with Joe eventually. Thatcher College was not that big and there were a limited number of hot guys to fuck.

Jessi hurried back to the dorm, wanting to shower and change into a new outfit for the evening before there was a chance Candi might bring Joe back to their room. She wanted to clear out before that happened.

Jogging across campus, Jessi could not help but smile at what had just happened. It was not that she had turned down the option for sex, but the fact she now felt more on equal terms with Candi. Her roommate had been a guide to her, but she was already feeling like she was catching up. Jessi still had a lot to learn about the college slut life, but she was excited to keep growing until she and Candi really were on the same level.

And it was a good thing Jessi hurried. Even rushing through a shower, she barely had time to change into a crop top and shorts, along with matching high heels, and apply an acceptable layer of makeup before Candi and Joe arrived.

"Have fun," Jessi said as she passed the soon to be happy couple in the hallway.

For the briefest of moments it seemed like Joe was going to suggest they both stay, but Jessi was glad to see that idea did not get spoken aloud. It was not that Jessi was against a three-way, but that she knew she was not ready for it yet.

"We will," Candi said, her voice laced with lust. Jessi was certain they were both going to have a good time.

However, once Jessi made it outside, she realized she had nowhere specific to go. There was a part of her that knew she should probably pay a visit to the library to catch up on the work she had missed so far. But her books were back in the dorm room and there was no way she was going to interrupt Candi's fun. Her roommate had made herself scarce for Jessi earlier in the week. Now it was Jessi's turn to go elsewhere while Candi got fucked with a hopefully big cock. She deserved it.

Jessi whipped out her phone and started dialing, realizing she really only had one option.

"Travis? It's Jessi. You free right now?"

There was a pause while Travis answered.

"I'll be right there. And just so you know, I've been practicing."

Despite wanting to give her throat a chance to recover, Jessi could think of nothing better to do than put her newly acquired skills to use. She was already licking her lips at the thought of taking Travis' impressive cock into her throat.

23

SHOPPING

Jessi stood in front of the mirror, looking at her reflection, studying it. She knew what she wanted to look like. She was close. She was very close. But she was not there yet. Her makeup application skills needed to improve, along with actually using more products to enhance her beauty and sexiness. Her clothes needed to get better too. Candi had shown her the way with her clothing and the simple problem was she needed more of her new style.

Licking her lips, Jessi focused on her mouth. Memories came flooding back to her from the night before when she had sucked Travis' cock. He had been impressed with how much she had improved from that first night at the party. Taking his impressive shaft down her throat had been an accomplishment by itself, but even now it turned her on to know how much she had pleasured him.

It also helped that Travis sent her the video. Jessi had watched it multiple times since. She loved the way she kept looking up at him, toward the camera, as she sucked his cock.

She loved the submissive look in her eyes. To her, it was the epitome of sexiness.

Travis had promised her that he would not send the video to anyone else, that he would not share it. Jessi had been thankful at the time, but in hindsight she wondered if maybe the video should be shared. It would certainly make Jessi a hotter commodity among the many hot men at Thatcher College. She doubted she would ever have to try that hard to find a man to suck or to fuck. The men would be more likely to seek her out when they were up for some fun.

"Damn, girl, you're looking fine," Candi said when she walked into the room to see Jessi examining her reflection. "Amy will be here in a minute to join us."

Jessi nodded her head, looking forward to it being more than just Candi who would be joining her at the mall. Amy was an established popular girl at Thatcher. Even though Candi was already miles ahead of Jessi in the hot slut department, she too was a new commodity on campus. Amy added an important perspective that would make sure Jessi still fit in with the vibe of the college.

Jessi smiled at Candi's compliment. She had worked extra hard on her most recent outfit, wanting it to be perfect for the trip to the mall. Then again, it was definitely hot and revealing. Jessi had managed to take a Thatcher College t-shirt and turn it into little more than a bandana that she tied around her boobs. Had she been bigger, the top would not have worked, or at least she would have needed an extra tie lower down along the triangle portion of the top, keeping it secured to her body so it did not flap up and reveal her tits.

The thong, short skirt, and heels completed the outfit, making Jessi look like she was ready to fuck at the drop of a hat. And in a way, she was. Not that sex was in her immediate plans. Even as she felt turned on from the memories from the day before, she also was aware that she could not keep up that kind of slutty behavior. It would be great for weekends, but for days when she had classes, it was a bit much. And she could not remain that sexed up. And still expect to pass her classes. That was still important.

"O-M-G," Amy squealed when she showed up at the door. "You look so hot."

"Thanks," Jessi said. "I like your tube top."

And she did. Jessi liked the way Amy's tits caused the small top to bulge around her tits. They almost looked fake with how round they appeared, but that was definitely a look Jessi could get behind. It was pretty clear that if Jessi ever wanted to be bigger, she would need to get implants. As small as she was, her options were limited. But at least, in the meantime, she could avoid worrying about bras.

After a round of hugs among the three friends, the trio soon found themselves at the mall for an afternoon of shopping. Jessi was tapping an emergency savings fund that had been given to her as a way to pay for emergencies, things like car repairs and the like. However, as far as Jessi was concerned, this shopping trip was an emergency. She could not continue being the hot slut that she was working to be unless she continued to revamp her wardrobe.

"Ooh, this is a hot pair," Amy said as they explored their first stop of the day. Amy needed more panties. The ones she had just were not going to continue to work for her. She had a few thongs, but she needed more. She even went further and bought skimpier styles, including one C-string that she wanted to try out. The strapless style would work well the next time she wore a dress or skirt that really could not otherwise be worn with underwear.

Once the underwear problem was solved, having collected enough pairs to make sure she could wear at least two pairs per day, the trio moved on to a makeup boutique that specialized in just the kinds of looks the three women preferred. The makeup that Jessi had received for her birthday had been a good start, but she now knew that there was room for so much more.

But the most important thing Jessi bought at the makeup boutique was a set of false lashes. Jessi had great eyes and she knew the best way to get people to notice them was if she made her eyes as eye-catching as possible. Long and thick lashes were just the answer and she could not wait for her next class with Cole. Her goal was to get him to fuck her. Kissing was great. So too was him feeling her up and possessively keeping his hand on her thigh during class. But she wanted to go all the way with him.

The three coeds ended up making multiple return trips to the car they came in as they quickly filled the trunk and then part of the back seat. Jessi bought shoes, lots of shoes, all of them sporting higher heels than she had ever considered before she met Candi and Amy. It had only been a few days, but she was already getting better at walking in them, almost forgetting that she was wearing them at all. They were becoming more and more natural feeling on her feet.

When it came to tops, Jessi found herself being very particular in what she purchased. Almost everything she bought needed to show off her belly-button. That was becoming more and more clear to her. She had no idea what she would do when winter finally came. The winter season could see several straight weeks below freezing. But then again, the Thatcher College campus was small enough that she would not need to spend much time outside between her classes. She could manage, as long as she bought a warm coat.

When it came to finishing her shopping trip, Jessi mostly stuck with skirts and shorts. She did buy a couple pairs of pants though. They were all tight as could be, acting as little more than tights, although they were definitely made to be seen. She also bought some tights too, but she planned to wear those as outerwear when needed. She saw little reason to cover up her body completely.

"Look at those," Amy squealed as they were making their way out of the mall. There was one last store that they had otherwise ignored. It was new and the staff were still setting up the window display, getting ready for an official weekend debut.

There were three mannequins in the window, all of them wearing club dresses that showed far more skin than they hid. But that was a desirable feature for the three coeds.

"Excuse me, are you open?" Jessi asked, poking her head through the main door.

"Technically yes," the shop clerk said. She was a young woman of college age. She had a lot in common with the three friends, although she was dressed far more conservatively, wearing a pair of black slacks and a blue polo with the store emblem on it. "But our real opening is tomorrow night."

"We saw the dresses on the mannequins," Candi said. "Just point us in the right direction and we'll take care of ourselves."

The clerk pointed toward the far corner of the store as she continued her work setting up the front window display. There were still boxes lying around on the floor, but the three friends were able to navigate through it all. Jessi was surprised that one girl had been left to set everything up, but she was not going to argue with her about it. She felt bad enough seeing her like that, without any help, while they were using their free time from classes to buy Jessi a new wardrobe.

In the end, each of the girls bought a new dress. Actually, Jessi bought two. They were both of a type that she would either need to wear her new C-string panties or go commando. But she was just fine with that. It was the hot slut thing to do. And that was what being a popular girl required. Not to mention, being a hot slut was a lot of fun. Jessi had only been at this for about a week, but she was already enjoying all the sex. She had never known sex could be that much fun.

Even though Jessi was still in the early stages of her new life, she could not help but feel for the store clerk. And from what Jessi saw, the girl had potential. She was stuck wearing her uniform, but that did not mean she was a drab kind of woman. If anything, the fact she was working at a store that sold the kind of clubbing dresses they were buying meant she had to have some style sense herself.

"Hey, if you're interested in partying this weekend at all, maybe after you close here, assuming you're working Saturday, you should give us a call," Jessi said.

She felt unnaturally bold as she did it, but she channeled the feeling she got from helping Candi with their workout yesterday to help her make the proposition. Jessi used the pen she had used to sign her receipt and grabbed a business card for the store manager. On the back she wrote her phone number and signed it Jessi, drawing a heart over the i.

"Thanks," the woman said. "I'm Elsa."

"Call me if you're interested," Jessi added with a wave before the trio left the lonely clerk to finish her preparations for the official store opening.

"Why'd you do that?" Amy asked. "She's probably a townie."

Jessi turned to look at her friend, her face surprisingly serious. "Did you see what her boss has her doing? Anyone who has to do all of that by herself deserves a break. Besides, she's cute and she had hot slut potential."

It was the first time Jessi had truly asserted herself with her friends. The workout with Candi had just been because she knew more about exercise than Candi. But this was something different. This was Jessi making a play to rise up the ranks of the popular girl clique.

And much to Jessi's surprise, Amy shrugged her shoulders and let it go. "You're probably right."

Jessi nearly stopped in shock at how Amy had just responded. But she managed to recover quickly enough to continue walking as if nothing had happened. But Jessi smiled to herself, knowing her place among the popular girls was becoming safer and safer with each passing day. She still had a lot to learn, but she had established herself as a force to be reckoned with on the Thatcher College campus.

2 4

SECOND THOUGHTS

As much as Jessi's stock was rising within the ranks of the popular girls on campus, she still had to deal with the men. For many of them, they were happy to help her grow into being a true hot slut, as was her current path. However, that was not true of everyone and Jessi still felt nervous about Cole.

Jessi knew Cole liked her. He had said as much at various times and his behavior toward her made it obvious that he wanted her. However, nothing was easy with Cole. And Cole had become Jessi's primary interest. Yes, the other men she had sex with were fun, but they were just a means to an end. They were to help her gain the experience she would need to eventually land and keep Cole. She wanted to be perfect for him.

And it was with that in mind that Jessi got up extra early for her Friday class with Cole. She did not even pay attention to what the class was anymore. It seemed unimportant. A part of her realized she was destined to fail the course, but she did her best to ignore that fact for the moment. To her, getting her outfit, hair, and makeup all right was more important. And as with Wednesday, she left early, wanting to get in as much make out time as possible before class started. It was the highlight of her day.

Jessi's outfit was a new one, something she bought on her shopping excursion the day before. She almost decided to wear her clubbing dress she bought from Elsa, but in the end she knew that needed to be saved for the weekend and the parties she would be attending. She hoped she could do so on Cole's arm. That would be the perfect way to spend her weekend. She was certain of that.

The outfit consisted of a cropped tank top over a pushup bra and a micro-mini skirt over a bright yellow G-string. She added a yellow cropped jacket that had no hope of actually closing, but it helped keep her arms warm in the cool morning air. Her shoes were high-heeled sandals. She could not walk very fast in them, but that only gave people more time to look at her and admire her fit and trim body. Jessi styled her hair to flow down her back in loose waves of blonde, bouncing behind her with each step she took.

The moment Jessi approached her first class, she spotted Cole already standing there, leaving against the wall.

"Were you waiting for me?" she cooed, unable to keep her voice from rising an octave as she walked up to him. Jessi immediately reached out and placed a hand on his muscled chest, barely covered in a tight t-shirt that squeezed around his perfect body. She imagined she could see his washboard abs through his shirt.

Cole looked at Jessi with a cool expression, unwilling to go too far in encouraging his latest interest. However, if there was any question about his current intentions with Jessi, he answered them by sliding his hand down around to her ass and giving it a squeeze.

Jessi shuddered in pleasure as Cole manhandled her. Her pussy grew wet and the fire of lust awakened inside of her. She had already been primed and was ready, but now it was happening, her body reacting to Cole's actions with fervor.

"Yeah, baby," Jessi said as Cole turned her around and pushed her up against the wall. She was reminded of her Wednesday fuck, but this was different, being out in the open.

However, the moment Cole's lips met Jessi's she became completely lost in the moment. Thoughts fled her mind as she was inundated with pleasure and desire. Cole could have done anything to her and she would have gone along with it. Her sense of self was entirely restricted to her actions with Cole. The location, the prospect of other students and of professors seeing them did not matter. Cole could have lifted her up and fucked her right there and she would have been perfectly happy.

Time lost all meaning as Cole kissed her. His hands romanced her body as his tongue explored her mouth. He claimed her with his lips, but it was his hands that drove Jessi wild with lust. He kept her pinned against the wall, but she was a willing participant. They moved over her body, taking special note of her breasts and her ass. But he even slid a hand underneath her short skirt and rubbed her pussy through the thin fabric of her panties. It would have been so easy for him to just tear them away and leave her bare down below.

Jessi would have loved that. She would have loved to have Cole take her, to use her body as he saw fit, to finally make her completely his in mind, body and soul. All that was needed was for him to take her the rest of the way, to finally use his big hard cock and push it into her wet and waiting pussy. It did not even need to be her pussy. Any of her holes would have done. She just wanted his cock. She needed his cock. Then everything in Jessi's life would be perfect.

Little did Jessi realize how much of a scene she and Cole created. Students walked by, focused on getting to their classes, but several stopped to stare, unable to get past the brazen sexuality of the moment. Even a few professors stopped, considering the idea of telling the two to either stop or find somewhere else to conduct a make out session. However, once it was clear that it was Cole, the starting quarterback of the football team, such ideas were left alone, not wanting to upset the balance of power athletes held on campus.

Eventually though, after what felt like ages, Cole broke the kiss. Somehow they had managed to continue to breathe throughout, but Jessi still felt short of air. Not that she minded. She was out of breath and completely infatuated with her crush.

"Come on," Cole said. "We need to get to class."

"Class?" Jessi said, confused. She had completely forgotten about their class. She was still focused on the moment, on the idea of Cole finally fucking her. That was what she wanted. That was what she needed.

Cole ignored Jessi's question as he grabbed her hand and pulled her into the classroom. All the other students had already taken their seats and the professor was already at his lectern, collecting his notes before he started into his lecture.

Jessi was unaware of all of this. More than ever, she was overwhelmed by the sexual feelings of lust and love that were welling up inside of her. That was not helped by Cole once again placing his hand on her thigh once they sat down. It was another ownership claim on her. She was his, whether he fully understood that or not.

And this time, in their third class together, his hand sat

even higher on her leg. If he pushed his hand any more between her legs, he would be rubbing her pussy through its thin cover.

Jessi's eyes were glassy as she looked up at Cole's face. He had his notebook out and he was taking notes with his free hand. Jessi never managed to even think about taking her own notebook out. She was lost in the lust that had overtaken her body and mind. Instead, she sat there, letting Cole's hand continue to drive her wild, forgetting that she was supposed to be a student.

Time continued to hold no meaning as Jessi continued to simply stare up at the god-like figure that she saw whenever she looked at Cole. Did he understand the power he held over her? Did he realize she would do absolutely anything he asked of her without question? She briefly realized he might be too focused on football to fully appreciate all that she had to offer.

However, the longer Jessi sat there, the more and more desperate she became. Forgetting that there was anyone else around, she started scooting closer to Cole. Her skirt rode up and soon her ass was fully touching the seat beneath her, only her little G-string keeping her from leaking her juices out onto the hard seat. But her real intention was to move Cole's fingers closer to her pussy. And it almost worked.

"Please," Jessi moaned quietly. It barely came out as a whisper, just loud enough for Cole to hear her.

She took hold of Cole's hand and pushed it deeper between her legs until his fingers were pressed up against her pussy.

Cole shot Jessi a sideways glance with a knowing smirk. He had seen this look, this reaction, from women before, although never before in such a public place. And he was certainly not going to leave Jessi completely wanting. His fingers began to dance between her legs, more teasing her than providing relief, but in Jessi's mind, they were really the same thing, leading to the same end. She was certain that she would soon have Cole's cock in her pussy where it belonged. That was her goal and she was certain it was coming.

As the other students in the class began to get up and put their notebooks away, Jessi finally regained some sense of the present. However, she was not particularly concerned with what she and Cole had done. She was far too horny for her to have any sense of shame. And that horniness was not going away anytime soon.

As Cole began to pack up his notebook, Jessi's voice returned to her. "How about we skip our next classes and have some fun?"

It was the most coherent thought Jessi had managed since Cole's hand first found her ass that morning, but she did not pay any attention to that fact. She was listening to her pussy and her pussy wanted to get fucked. She needed it more than anything.

Cole took a moment to look Jessi up and down. Even he had to admit she looked hot and she was definitely willing. However, she was still lacking in several important areas. Until then, he was just going to have to enjoy the potential she held. That was until she became the woman he wanted her to be. But that would take time and serious commitment on her part. Cole had met women who were close. He had fucked them, but they had never been more than a good fuck. He wanted Jessi to be more than that though.

"You're not ready yet," Cole finally said.

"But…"

However, Cole was already walking away. Jessi sat there, staring at his perfect ass as he tossed a football in his hands. He paused at the door, looking over his shoulder. He flashed her a smile, as if that made it all better. Then he disappeared out of sight.

Jessi sat there for a long time, her fingers lightly tracing her clit through her panties, her hands acting of their own accord, keeping her mind full of mostly mush. The one thought that kept rattling around in her head was a question. What did she need to do to be ready for him?

MAKING A DEAL

Was it a rejection or a call to action? That was what dominated Jessi's thoughts as she floated through her morning. Her remaining classes were just a blur of worry and arousal. Cole told her she was not ready yet. Did he want her to be ready? He seemed intent on making out with her before class. He pushed her to the edge during class, keeping his hand on her thigh, getting achingly close to her pussy. He had to see potential in her. But potential for what? What did Jessi need to do to be ready for him?

Jessi was late to her next class, although not nearly as late as she had been Wednesday. That was because there was no guy to fuck. She saw no one who could satisfy her urges, her lust. Jessi knew she needed a good pounding. Until then, she would not be able to think straight.

Deep down, Jessi knew she was on the cusp of something. She was aware that her poor attention in class would quickly come back to bite her. This was Friday, the last day of her first week of her sophomore year at Thatcher College. She bad barely managed to take any notes. She did not even know her professors' names. Those all got lost in her over-sexed mind. And yet, despite knowing there was a problem, she could not bring herself to change anything.

No, Jessi was having far too much fun being a hot slut, with a special emphasis on the slut part. But more than anything, she was finding herself growing into a role that she was quickly adopting, even finding girls who were already popular and hot sluts in their own rights had started to look to her for leadership. It was strange, especially considering how inexperienced Jessi really was.

However, as Jessi eventually found herself sitting in her third and final class of the day, she was lost in the fog of her own arousal. Cole had completely ruined her for complex thought. The only thing that could save her from her lust was an orgasm. But it was not as if she could easily take care of that while in class. Then again, Candi's rules of men, then women, and only then self had been fully drilled into Jessi's head. A bathroom break was not in her future. She needed to wait to fulfill her needs.

Jessi sat there, her eyes unfocused, imagining the size of the cocks in the classroom. This particular class was seated around a large square of tables. She could see all the other students and especially the professor. It was the same professor who kept her after class last time, who suggested a more intimate relationship might be in order to help her pass. Given her current situation, that sounded like a grand idea.

Even though Jessi's eyes remained glazed throughout the class discussion, talking about a book Jessi had not bothered to read, she remained aware every time the professor looked in her direction. She automatically licked her lips whenever he looked her way. It was an unconscious response, one that she was not aware of, but it affected the professor greatly. He definitely could not avoid looking in her direction and he opted to remain seated throughout the class period to avoid revealing the bulge in his pants.

Despite it feeling as if class was taking forever, Jessi found herself surprised when her classmates were packing up their notebooks. It was enough to shake her out of her lust-ridden fog, at least a little bit. Her eyes refocused enough to see that the women she had sat beside both gave her disgusted looks. They were clearly unhappy sitting next to a hot and slutty girl, someone who used their looks to get by instead of her mind. However, Jessi saw it as them being jealous. They are jealous of her hot body and all the men she could attract.

However, Jessi did not move to leave with the rest of her classmates. The look she got from her professor kept her in her seat. She could tell that he wanted to talk to her, that he might have further information to give her about his proposal.

"Jessi," the professor said. "I'm glad you weren't as late to class today, but if you're not going to pay attention in class, we're going to need to come to another arrangement. Why don't you join me in my office and we can discuss your options?"

Jessi simply nodded her head, not being in any condition to answer properly. However, the moment the professor rose to his feet, Jessi's gaze locked onto his crotch. She saw the bulge in his pants. She again found herself licking her lips, her mind automatically thinking about what it would be like to have his package in her mouth, testing her gag reflex that she had been working to suppress. And if he could fuck her too, all the better.

"Come with me," the professor said as he collected his notebook and started for the door.

Jessi obediently got up from her seat and followed him

out of the classroom. It was a short walk to his office. A part of Jessi felt like she was in trouble. After all, she had not been doing what she was supposed to do. She was not paying attention in class. In high school, that would have meant detention, which she had never needed to suffer through. She had always followed the rules and never gotten in trouble. But getting led back to the professor's office made her feel like she was in trouble, except in a far more pleasant way.

She knew what was likely to happen next. Jessi was fully aware of the kind of proposal the professor wanted to make her. And despite the inherent naughtiness of it, she wanted it. She needed it. Such a relationship would cement her position among the hot sluts, making her role as a popular girl at Thatcher College secure. She just had to hope that the professor's reach was large enough so that she could truly live up to her hot slut potential. After all, she needed to ready herself for Cole.

"Shut the door, please," the professor said as Jessi followed him into his office.

She did exactly as she was told, even taking an extra few seconds to close the door quietly. Jessi was generally aware of the college guidelines that barred one-on-one meetings between students and professors behind closed doors, unless the subject of the discussion needed to remain private. Then again, Jessi was certain this discussion would need to be private, given what was going to be discussed.

"You seem determined not to pay attention in my class," the professor said, taking a hardline approach to start the conversation. He walked around and sat behind his desk, motioning for Jessi to take a seat across from him.

Jessi took the offered seat and squeezed her thighs together, trying to fight off another wave of arousal. She needed to maintain some semblance of rationality as she discussed what could possibly be a very lucrative deal for her, assuming she and the professor were on the same page.

"It's hard," Jessi admitted. "I'm just so horny when I get to your class."

"Then I think I have an idea of how I can help you," the professor said. "Come around the desk and get down on your knees."

Jessi did not need telling twice. She popped up out of her seat and minced around the desk in her high heels. She then sank gracefully to her knees, right in front of the professor. His cock was already out, big, hard, and throbbing. Just the sight of it was enough to make Jessi's mouth water. That was a new sensation, to be so looking forward to having a cock in her mouth that she would salivate over it, but it was not unwelcome. Then again, she figured it was just because she was so horny.

Jessi took her professor's cock into her mouth, using her tongue to make sure he was completely hard for her. She wanted, no needed, to taste his cum. That was her goal. She needed to make him cum. She needed him to feed her lunch.

"Touch yourself," the professor said as Jessi bobbed her head on his cock, taking more and more of his cock into her mouth each time.

Jessi did not answer with his cock in her mouth, but she did as he instructed. She pulled her short skirt up around her waist, revealing the small thong she wore beneath it. Her long-nailed fingers slipped beneath the thin fabric and began to slowly circle her clit. She could not let her own ministrations disrupt the blowjob and distract her from her real purpose, which was to give her professor as much pleasure as he could handle. That was how she was going to save her grade.

"Oh, that's nice," the professor moaned as he sat back and enjoyed the work of the hot little blonde in front of him. If this was his first time with a student, it did not show. Not that Jessi cared one way or another. She just liked the fact he had a big cock and he could help her avoid the double work of keeping her grades up and satisfying her growing libido and need to be popular.

There was a small voice in Jessi's head that told her this was wrong. However, she had a hard time deciding what the voice really meant. Did it mean that sucking off a professor for a favorable grade was wrong or that fingering herself to get off was wrong when she had a cock in front of her? Either way, Jessi pushed back against that voice, not wanting to listen to it. She felt too good to give credence to the voice. This was what she wanted to be doing and who she wanted to be. That was what mattered.

With her pent up arousal, Jessi's fingers soon had her ever so close to cumming. However, she managed to hold back, not wanting to cum before the professor was ready himself. But she could sense he was getting close. His moans had turned into groans as he threw his head back and shut his eyes in erotic ecstasy. She kept an eye upward, watching her professor's reactions to her blowjob skills. He seemed especially to enjoy it when she dove down onto his cock fully, taking him into her throat. It was easier for her than ever before.

"Sit back," he suddenly said, shocking Jessi. He even pushed gently on her forehead, pushing her back, off of his cock, but only inches away.

Jessi looked up in confusion to see him looking down on her with a lust-filled gleam in his eyes. His hands fell to his cock as he started jacking himself.

"Cum for me," he ordered.

And Jessi did. She finally let her orgasm take her. And it was glorious. Her whole body sang out in erotic ecstasy. But it was more than that. The professor's cock sent out its first surge of cum, hitting her in the face. It was not her first facial, but she did not mind in the slightest that the professor wanted to paint her face with his cum. It was like a mark of ownership. Not that the professor owned her, but she would do anything to make their arrangement more lucrative for the both of them.

"So good," Jessi moaned as she started to come down off her orgasm, her body recovering from the total body effects of her special moment with the professor.

"You are good," the professor agreed. "You're very good. And I definitely think we should be making this a regular part of our student-professor relationship. It will at least make up for you not being worth a damn in my class."

Jessi nodded her head, her face still covered in cum, foreseeing how this could indeed become a fortuitous relationship. But she wanted more. Blowjobs were nice, especially when she could play with herself as she had, but she wanted more from him. At the very least, she wanted to be fed his cum, if he did not actually fuck her.

"But if you're really interested in me helping you pass not just my class, but your other classes, we're going to have to advance this relationship a bit more. Would you like that?"

"Yes, please," Jessi answered, her face still covered in cum. She had not moved to clean it off her face, although she was looking forward to licking as much of it up as possible.

The professor smiled. "I thought you might like that. While you clean up your face, why don't I figure out a good time for our next meeting. I don't want to take you away from your weekend parties, but Sunday should probably work. How does that sound?"

"It sounds perfect," Jessi said with a cum covered smile. She started licking her lips. Then she pulled a piece of cloth from her purse and began to wipe her face clean. She chose the cloth because she could lick the cum from it, making for a small snack before she joined her friends for lunch. Assuming they were still at the dining hall. Jessi had been delayed long enough that she might have missed them.

As Jessi cleaned up her face, the professor pulled out one of his business cards and wrote down both his home address and a time for Sunday's rendezvous. He was looking forward to it, having already seen what Jessi was capable of when using her mouth and lips. But he wanted to get the whole taste of her. Blowjobs in his office were fine, but he wanted more and that meant her coming to his house for some extracurricular studying.

As soon as Jessi was mostly put back together again, although with a need to fully retouch her makeup, the professor handed her the card.

"Be at that address on Sunday," he said. "And don't forget."

"I won't, professor," Jessi said.

"Mmm, I like that," He said. "From now on, you're always to call me either Professor or Sir. Understood?"

"Yes, Sir," Jessi answered automatically. She could definitely call him those things if he wanted.

"Good. You can see yourself out. I'll see you at my home on Sunday."

"Yes, Sir," Jessi said as she returned to her feet and made sure her skirt was properly covering her body again. Then she swayed her hips as she walked out, giving her ass a little extra wiggle as she opened the office door to leave.

It was only as Jessi was walking across campus toward the dining hall a minute later that she looked down at the card clutched in her hand. Her professor's name was Octavius Wright. That was good to know. She felt silly for not remembering her professors' names, but she had been so preoccupied since starting classes that their names had slipped her mind. But Professor Wright was soon becoming her favorite professor, mostly because he was willing to fuck her. And in return, she might not need to worry about her grades.

"Hey, girlfriends," Jessi said as she walked into the dining hall to join her friends. She smiled, knowing how much they were going to enjoy the story of her latest escapades.

A PERFECT FRIDAY AFTERNOON

J essi gave her friends a complete rundown on what had just transpired. Amy and the other popular girls looked at her with awe. Yes, they had been rumored to have slept with professors for grades before, but none of them had actually done it. They had just let those rumors spread, knowing that it increased their hot slut credibility.

Candi, however, smiled and looked on at her roommate with pride, seeing what she had helped to create. It had only been about a week, but Jessi had come amazingly far. And she knew this was just the beginning. There was so much more that Jessi would get to experience before her time at Thatcher College was over. The hard part was figuring out exactly when that would be. Candi had high hopes for Jessi, but she knew she was playing with fire. Jessi would need to leave the college eventually, whether by choice or by necessity.

By the time lunch was over, Jessi had her fill of sharing her story, as well as her fill of food. And after an eventful morning, she found herself getting tired and needing a nap.

"A nap sounds really good right now," Candi said as she

saw Jessi yawn. "We've got parties to attend tonight. Catching up on some rest now means more fun tonight."

Jessi nodded her head in agreement. That did sound good to her. She had no idea what parties were planned, but she had a feeling she would not be seeing Cole out and about. He had a game tomorrow. Jessi had no doubt he would be in bed early and doing his best to prepare for the game, making it a big win. Or so she hoped. Jessi had little experience with sports, never caring before. However, if she wanted to eventually get with Cole, she knew she needed to go to his games. If only she understood football at all.

Once back in their room, both Jessi and Candi quickly tucked themselves into bed, catching a little sack time before they needed to be up and alert later. After everything that had happened already in her day, she was ready for some sleep. And when sleep finally did take her, it was with a smile on her lips. It had been a good day, between making out with Cole and giving Professor Wright a blowjob. And now Jessi was getting a little rest before her day—and night—kicked up into even higher gear.

Even though Jessi had no idea how her evening would unfold, she was certain there would be parties and drinking. And her understanding of the rest of the weekend told her it would also be heavily influenced by parties and alcohol. She found it hard to believe that she had only started drinking a few days ago, but she was already looking forward to a booze-filled weekend with lots of hot guys and sex.

However, after what amounted to a two-hour nap, neither Jessi nor Candi were ready to do a whole lot with their afternoon. Instead, they texted Amy and the others to see if they wanted to spend the rest of the afternoon out on the quad, sunning themselves. Amy volunteered to smuggle out some vodka, which Jessi thought was a grand idea. As long as she kept hydrating in addition to getting her afternoon buzz on, she was all for it.

Before they knew it, the crew of popular girls were all laying out on towels in the grass on the quad, wearing bikinis and sunglasses, sipping water from water bottles, but passing an extra bottle around that Amy had filled with vodka. It did not take long before they were gossiping and generally having a good time under the September sun, all the while working on their tans as they wore tiny bikinis that barely covered their bodies.

Jessi especially enjoyed herself as she watched a group of what she assumed were fraternity brothers toss a football around. They were not actual football players, although they might have played in high school. No, they were just fit and generally handsome guys enjoying themselves on a sunny Friday afternoon.

Before all of this had started, she had never considered herself particularly boy crazy, although she had to admit she had missed that phase when she was younger. Now her eyes automatically tracked them as they ran around with their shirts off, exposing six-pack abs that they probably spent all summer working on. Who knew if they were going to be able to keep them during the school year, but Jessi could hope.

Given her past, Jessi was left completely unable to fully understand how her mind seemed fixated on men. Even after her earlier exploits, she found herself almost salivating over the guys playing catch, following every movement they made as their skin practically glowed from the sweat sheen. And more than that, Jessi found herself wondering what they were packing, how big their cocks were. Such a thing had never been important before, but after spending time with so many large cocks, that was all she wanted anymore.

"I bet you're hungry for another man between your legs,"

Amy commented as she spotted how Jessi's gaze seemed fixated on the football throwing frat boys.

Without even thinking about it, Jessi nodded her head in agreement. She was not sure what it was, but Amy was right. Jessi was becoming an insatiable slut. Given her earlier exploits, she should have been satisfied, but she was already getting wet again. She did not understand it at all, but the arousal felt good. That certainly helped her mood, keeping a smile on her face.

"Save it for tonight," Candi said. "Trust me."

Jessi nodded again. She was not sure she could last that long, but she did trust her roommate. Candi had yet to lead her astray. If anything, she had been a great role model and mentor for her.

"That's nothing better than being drunk and horny," Amy said just before she took another swig from the water bottle filled with vodka.

Thatcher College's response to student drinking was remarkably liberal compared to many campuses. The administration knew students would drink. Pushing them to always do it off campus and to hide it was just asking for more trouble and more irresponsible behavior. But by allowing it on campus, asking students to do it behind closed doors, in their rooms, making it private, students could experiment in relative safety.

However, what Amy, Jessi, Candi, and the others were doing was still against the rules. The clear liquid looked just like water. And since they were not causing any disturbances, no one minded that they were slowly working their way into an inebriated state on the campus quad. And Jessi was definitely feeling the effects of the alcohol. Her head felt like it was floating, her mind already muddled under the intoxicating effects. And somehow that only made her more aroused. She wanted nothing more than to touch herself through her brief bikini bottoms.

And as soon as Amy finished her sip, the bottle got passed around again, finding its way to Jessi. She took more than a sip, already rolling into the rest of her night, knowing it was going to be fun. And Jessi had already learned that the highlight of any party was a fun and drunk party girl. That was who she was going to be tonight, regardless of where she ended up.

Eventually the sun started to get too low in the sky to keep up the pretense of tanning. It was hard to say whether any of them actually picked up any additional color, but none of them regretted the chance to lay around on the quad for all to see. If anything, it was an advertisement for later, telling all of the eligible men on campus that they were going to be needed as the hot sluts hit the Friday night parties.

The moment Jessi pushed herself to her feet, she stumbled, her balance thrown off by her level of inebriation.

"Fuck, I'm drunk," she said, her words slightly slurred. That was more to do with her numb lips and face than it was to actually how drunk she was. Once she found her balance, however, Jessi started giggling to herself, finding the whole situation to be humorous.

"Looks like we've got a bimbo on our hands," Amy said as she reached out to steady her friend.

Jessi was not exactly sure what Amy meant, but she kept right on giggling. Eventually Candi took the place of Amy and the pair stumbled into their dorm and up to their shared room.

"Am I a bimbo?" Jessi asked as she plopped down onto her bed. She tried to pout, but as her body bounced on the mattress, she started giggling again. She had been drunk before, but she had never been so giggly like this before.

"Not yet you're not," Candi said as she untied her bikini

and started searching through her wardrobe for her next outfit.

Jessi continued to sit on her bed, still wearing her bikini, not yet moving to change for dinner.

"Should I be a bimbo?" Jessi asked.

"If you want," Candi answered. "Some guys are into that. But while bimbos are known for being super sexy and often slutty, much like you are, they are also known to be pretty dumb. Big boobs help too."

Jessi looked down at her chest. Her small breasts barely pushed out the triangles of her bikini top. She simply did not have much in the chest department, unlike Candi who had an impressive pair of tits. And those were all natural. Candi had simply won the genetic lottery when it came to breast development. But seeing her now, Jessi felt a pang of jealousy ring through her. She wanted to be as sexy as possible and it was clear that guys found bigger boobs sexier. It was simple math that even a drunk and aroused coed could complete.

"Hey," Candi said, seeing Jessi grow despondent. "There are remedies to that sort of thing, but you shouldn't worry about that right now. Yes, a lot of guys like bigger boobs, but that hasn't stopped anyone from fucking you yet. There's more to life than just being a sexy slam piece. And to be honest, most guys have low standards. You're already flying high above those."

Jessi looked up at Candi and a smile slowly returned to her face. "Thanks," she finally added, already feeling better. She pushed herself up and started sorting through her own wardrobe, not only looking for an outfit to wear to dinner, but trying to decide what she was going to wear for their night out. It was going to be a good night.

However, even as Jessi focused on preparing herself for her night of fun, she could not stop thinking about what it would be like to be a bimbo. She wondered what it would be like to have big boobs. She wondered what it would be like to be dumb. There was a part of her that was intrigued. There was a part of her that found the whole concept arousing. She wondered if Cole would be into that sort of thing. But more importantly, would he want her to be a bimbo for him?

By the time she finished changing into an outfit worthy of going to dinner, her mind had already moved onto other things, the idea of becoming a bimbo forgotten in her inebriation. But there was no doubt that Jessi would be faced with the concept of being a bimbo again. Given her drive to be hot and popular, it was bound to come up again.

SWEDISH FUN

Jessi could hear the beat of the music from outside the house as she stumbled up the steps. She was with the rest of the popular crew, all of them dressed like sluts with one thing on their minds. Jessi was still feeling the effects of the alcohol in her bloodstream. But that was kind of the idea.

After sobering up a bit over dinner, Jessi had resumed her drinking afterward, wanting to make sure she was nice and buzzed when she hit the first party of the night. However, once the other girls showed up to pregame for the night, it all got a little out of hand. Jessi quickly lost track of how many drinks she had consumed—not that she was counting to begin with, but she had been trying to keep a general idea of the number—and that led her to her current situation.

It would have been easy to blame her stumbles on the high heels she wore or the way she kept having to pull down her skirt to keep it from sliding up over her butt and revealing her lack of panties to anyone who happened to be nearby. She had planned to wear panties, but had forgotten when she changed into her party outfit for the night.

Luckily, Jessi had her friends there to support her. Amy and Candi, both intoxicated themselves, managed to catch Jessi before she hit the front porch of the house. All three started giggling in response, unable to control themselves. They all knew it was going to be a good night.

The whole group got waved in through the front door, getting to ignore the cover charge the hosts were charging for cups. Hot sluts like them never paid for their drinks like that. And skipping that little part of the process meant they were able to swarm the dance floor much sooner than normal.

Jessi let the beat of the music take hold of her as she started to dance with her friends. She had never been much of a dancer before, but she did not need to be. Between her inebriation and the steady beat of the music, she was able to move her body on instinct, letting the music carry her movements. And when she got a little lost, when a moment of lucidity returned to her mind, all she had to do was look to her friends and copy their grinding movements.

After the first song dancing with each other, the various men at the party started to make their moves. Candi, having the biggest boobs of the group, was the first to pair off with a man. She got first pick and she chose well, snagging a handsome man with broad shoulders and lots of muscles, barely covered in a tight shirt. Jessi could only guess what he was packing in his pants, but she knew Candi would be sure to leave him more than satisfied and hopefully he would be able to return the favor.

Amy was next. She was the most known hot slut on campus. Even if Jessi had never known her name before she embarked on this journey to become one of the popular girls, she had seen her on campus and was generally aware of what she did when she was not in class. When she paired off with another handsome man, one that she had been with multiple times in the past, it was obvious how the night was going to end for her. She was going to be screaming his name as he railed her with his big hard cock.

However, what Jessi was not expecting was for her to be next. She had kept an eye on the door, as well as the stairs leading up to the second floor, just in the slim hope that she would see Cole. Not that she had a hope of scoring with him yet. In his words, she was not ready yet, but she could still hope. Of course, what was left of her rational side knew he would not be there. He had a football game to prepare for. He would not be a good player if he was out partying the night before the first game of the season.

However, with no Cole, Jessi knew it would be someone else. And as it turned out, it was someone she never would have expected. There was no doubt that Jessi had developed a taste for athletic men. She had a crush on the starting quarterback, but Travis was a basketball player and her impromptu fuck Wednesday morning in an empty classroom had been with a soccer player. Only Jonas and Professor Wright were not athletes.

"Mind if I dance with you?" the man asked as he approached. Jessi looked up his body, her gaze starting at his muscular shoulders and moving up to his green eyes. His hair was long, coming down to his jaw. He looked vaguely familiar, but between the current situation and her intoxication, she could not place him. All Jessi knew was that the man was hot and he wanted to dance with her.

"Sure thing, baby," she said, barely able to keep herself from slurring her words. She brought her hands up and placed them on the man's chest, feeling his muscles beneath his shirt. He was strong. That much was clear to Jessi.

"My name is Christof," the man said.

That was enough to jog Jessi's memory. Christof was a foreign student known both for his musical and acting talents. She was vaguely aware that he was on scholarship for both. He regularly performed concerts, specializing in the piano, but he was also part of almost every theater production, and he was rumored to be writing his own musical that would be put on in the spring.

There was also some memory, buried deep down in Jessica's memory bank, of Christof being madly in love with a woman from his home country of Sweden, but that was not going to stop Jessi from acting in her own self interest. She had no qualms with getting involved with Christof, even if he was in a committed relationship. It was her own fault for not being there. Besides, it was just sex. It was not like Jessi was planning to steal Christof away permanently.

"I'm Jessi," she answered as she reached up and wrapped her arms around the back of Christof's neck. His hands slid down her body and found purchase on her hips where he could guide her as they danced to the currently playing slow song.

"You must be new around here," he said. "I think I'd remember someone like you from past years."

Jessi let out a drunken giggle, not wanting to explain anything about her past. If people wanted to believe she was new to Thatcher College, she was not going to dispel them of that notion. Besides, it was easier when she was not carrying around the baggage of her past nerdy and boring life. She was a popular girl now. She was a hot slut. She was Jessi, not Jessica.

After the slow song, the next song was faster and with a much stronger base line. Jessi turned around and started grinding her ass into Christof. His hands first held her hips, but they slid up to her shoulders as he pushed back against her ass. But then his hands eventually found purchase on her boobs. Jessi was already aroused and looking for sex, but

Christof's hands sent a bolt of pleasure into her body, sending her arousal skyrocketing.

"Do you wanna go someplace and have some fun?" Jessi asked after the song ended. She punctuated her question by pushing herself up on her toes and stealing a kiss. It was short, but there was enough tongue involved to make it clear what her intentions were.

"Sounds like fun," Christof answered. His English was nearly perfect. He was a senior and his three years on campus had allowed him to almost completely lose his accent. All of that theater training had played a major role in teaching him how to speak like his fellow students and otherwise blend in. "But let's get a drink first."

Jessi nodded her head as Christof took her by the hand and led her toward the kitchen. She had already had plenty to drink, but she was not going to pass up a chance to have a drink with Christof. Besides, at her current level of inebriation, what was one more drink? She just wanted to fit in and be the hot slut that was about to get laid.

There was a keg in the kitchen, but Christof ignored the keg and instead began to raid the cabinets. Jessi had no idea what he was doing, but before she knew it, she was holding a plastic cup filled with a blue cocktail. Even as drunk as she already was, she could smell the booze within the drink.

"It's a Polar Bear from my country," Christof explained. "Why don't we head up to my room now so we can get better acquainted?"

Jessi tested her drink, taking a small sip. It was good. She was certain it was much better than the beer in the keg. But more importantly, she had no idea that Christof lived in the house and was one of the party hosts. It was one thing to commandeer a bedroom for a little fun, but it was even better when her partner for the night actually owned the bedroom.

Smiling, Jessi let herself be led upstairs and into a previously locked bedroom. Christof flipped on the light to reveal what amounted to an average college man's bedroom. There were posters on the wall, including several theater posters for plays he had been in. There were also a couple posters that included scantily clad women, which was expected. What Jessi did not see, however, was any indication that Christof had a girlfriend back home. There were no bedside photos or anything else that told her he was taken. It made her feel all the better about what she was going to do.

Jessi found herself sitting on the bed with Christof beside her. They chatted as they drank, talking about nothing in particular. They were just going through the motions, getting ready for what was going to come next.

She looked down to see Christof slide his hand onto her bare thigh. It immediately reminded her of Cole, but Christof's touch was different. It was softer and less possessive. And it was only when Jessi looked over toward Christof that she realized her hand was gently stroking the bulge in Christof's pants. He was hard and his cock felt big. However, she would only know for certain when he took off his pants.

The drinks were good and strong, making sure there was no chance that Jessi's body had the opportunity to process all of the alcohol already in her system. There might have been a time when she would have accused Christof of trying to get her drunk so she would sleep with him, but that had always been her goal. The alcohol just made her even more of the fun and drunk party girl that she was for the night. This was all a part of her plan, as much as she had a plan. Getting fucked was the real goal and it was clear that was about to happen.

"I want you," Christof said. "You are so hot and sexy."

Jessi chugged down the rest of her drink. Formalities, like sharing a drink together, had been completed. But now it was time for the main event. If she remembered, she was going to have to get the cocktail recipe from Christof at some point. Such questions, however, could wait. She had more pressing concerns to deal with.

Christof set the rest of his drink aside and made his move. The moment their lips met again, Jessi pulled him in close and nearly pulled him over, no longer able to keep her own balance. They tumbled back onto the bed as they continued to kiss. Their tongues danced in each other's mouths, exploring and intertwining.

But as Jessi focused on the kissing, Christof's hands roamed, pushing up Jessi's skirt. He paused when he discovered she was not wearing panties.

"Naughty girl," he mumbled as his hands continued their work. All the while, he never broke the kiss they shared together.

Jessi's mind went fuzzy as her body prepared for the sexual pleasure of the act she was about to commit. She would never remember helping to remove Christof's clothes, nor would she remember how her own clothes came off. But she was certainly not complaining when Christof pushed his hard cock into her wet and waiting pussy.

"Fuck yes," she called out as he thrust into her for the first time, giving her a much needed filling. It had been too long since she last had a cock in her pussy. In her state, she could not manage to count how longer that was, but it was too long by her newly slutty standards.

"You are such a slut," Christof groaned as he set up a rhythm.

"Such a slut," Jessi repeated. "Fuck me like a slut. Fuck me hard. Come on, harder."

Christof certainly was not going to turn her down. His sensual nature was replaced by strength and speed, the kind Jessi had come to learn was common among the athletes on campus. Christof might be the sensual lover, but right now she just wanted to get fucked hard. She wanted to be fucked like a slut.

Of course, such hard fucking comes at a cost. Just as a start that burns brightest burns out the fastest, a fuck like Christof gave to Jessi could not last for long. Christof came, unannounced, his cock throbbing inside of her and shooting his hot white cum deep into her pussy. Jessi screamed out as her orgasm fired through her, stronger than anything she had felt before, permanently marking her for the slut that she was becoming.

Once done, Christof pulled out and collapsed onto the bed beside Jessi. He turned his head to look at her smiling face. Jessi looked back and felt pure joy and contentment. If there was any question as to whether she had made the right choice in turning herself into a slut to become popular, that moment cemented her answer. The answer was yes.

"If you give me a few moments," Christof said, his chest rising and falling with the deep breaths needed to recover from his previous exertions, "I'll be able to go again."

Jessi nodded her head, liking the sound of that. But then an idea came to her, somehow managing to fight through the post-orgasmic fog and inebriation. She could get him ready sooner with a little help.

Without saying a word, Jessi pushed herself up off the bed and positioned herself between Christof's legs. His cock was soft, clearly spent. However, she still took him into her mouth and did everything she could to get him hard again. Her night was not going to end there. She wanted so much more. It was time to fully embrace her slutty side and embrace the wanton sexuality of her new life. This was a part of being popular and it was so much fun. Christof certainly was not complaining. It was going to be a good night.

2 8

WALK OF SHAME

The moment Jessi woke up, she knew she was not in her own bed. The sheets felt different, more coarse. And there was a warmth beside her, a man.

Jessi opened her eyes slowly, wary of her head, knowing she had consumed far too much alcohol the night before. However, she had somehow managed to avoid a hangover, at least so far. Now she just had to figure out where she was.

Turning her head, Jessi found herself face to face with a sleeping Christof. His eyes were closed and he looked just as handsome as she remembered from the night before. She certainly had no regrets about all the fun the pair had the night before, as well as into the early morning. In fact, Jessi had half a mind to wake him up for another round. His cock had felt so good inside of her and she was already aching for more.

An intermittent buzzing sound interrupted Jessi's thoughts as she had been trying to decide between sneaking underneath the covers for a covert blowjob or waking Christof up for a proper ride on his cock. It took a moment for Jessi to connect the buzzing sound with her phone. She had somehow managed to bring it along with her to the party, hidden away in her tiny outfit.

Still naked from the night before, Jessi flopped halfway off the bed, reaching for her discarded clothing on the floor and the source of the buzzing. As soon as she picked up the phone, she knew it was Candi. She just had a feeling, especially after staying out all night with a guy. Not that Jessi had any regrets.

"Get your slutty ass back to the room," Candi texted. She fired the texts off in single sentences.

"We gotta get ready for tailgating."

"Enjoy the walk of shame, hot stuff."

Jessi quickly typed out a reply, telling her roommate that she was on her way.

"Where you going?" Christof asked as he wrapped an arm around Jessi, pulling her back toward him in bed. "You're leaving already?"

"I gotta go," Jessi said. However she punctuated her statement with a kiss on Christof's lips. If she was not such a slut, she probably could have found herself falling for him. He was different from most of the other men she hooked up with. The foreign influence made him fun. But there was no doubt that Jessi had a thing for athletes. And besides, her goal was still to land Cole. She wanted to be perfect for him, but she needed more experience. She needed more than experience, but Cole had not filled her in on the details yet.

"No time for a quickie?" Christof asked. It was clear that he wanted nothing more than to lay around in bed all morning with Jessi. In truth, she wanted that too. However, she knew she had places to go and people to see.

In truth, Jessi did not know what tailgating was. It was a foreign term to her. She was aware of what it actually was, the partying and drinking that took place before football games. She just did not know that it had a specific name.

At the mention of sex, Jessi immediately got wet, her body craving another round with Christof. She glanced at the time on her phone. It still seemed early enough. Candi never gave her a timeline and if she was going to live up to her slut image, she really needed to start her day off right.

"We have to make it quick," Jessi said as she rolled over and straddled Christof. His cock was already hard. It took little effort to position herself above him and then sink down onto his throbbing cock. It continued to throb inside of Jessi as she began to buck and grind against him.

Christof's hands went up to Jessi's small breasts and began to knead them and use his big hands to swallow them up. Fireworks went off behind Jessi's eyes as pleasure shot through her body. Normally, Jessi's control from being on top would have allowed her to extend their latest fuck session for as long as possible, but speed really was of the essence. She worked hard to bring him off, feeling her own orgasmic energy building.

And even through Christof had cum more times than he could probably count the night before, his cock was ready for a quick morning fuck. It took little time before he was flooding Jessi's body with his hot white cum. And as his seed splashed inside of her, Jessi was cumming too. It was not the grand orgasms that had rocked her body the night before, the kind that left her panting and barely able to function for several minutes.

This was smaller, but just as pleasant. It was exactly what she needed to get her day started. And as she climbed off Christof, his cum dribbling out of her pussy, she wondered if she could arrange a morning fuck every morning. It was certainly invigorating and put a happy smile on her face.

"Put your number in my phone," Jessi said, tossing Christof her phone as she started to pull on her clothes. Not that it was difficult to dress herself. The short skirt and tiny top were all she wore, besides the high heels. "I'll text you and we can do this again sometime. I'm always looking for friends like you."

"Sure thing," Christof said as she started a new contact for himself in her phone. He glanced through the other contacts. He recognized a few of the names listed in her contacts as prominent athletes on campus. He had no idea she was as big of a slut as she was. Not that Christof minded. As far as he was concerned, this was the way to get over his ex. She did not like the distance. Neither had Christof, but now he did not need to worry about that. There were a bevy of coeds available to him now and he planned to sample more than just Jessi.

Once Jessi had her shoes on, she took back her phone and gave Christof another kiss. If she was not so hung up on Cole and determined to be a hot slut, she would have readily given herself over to Christof. He was a nice guy with a big cock. And he definitely knew how to use that cock. Jessi had learned a lot from him and he had filled her in ways she had absolutely loved. But she had higher aspirations and there was only one man she was willing to get tied down to and that was Cole.

Walking across campus toward the dorm, Jessi felt the cool morning air against her exposed skin. Her inner thighs were especially cold as Christof's cooling seed slowly dripped out of her pussy. She would have to clean up when she got back to her dorm room. On the way, she texted Christof, thanking him for the fun night and making sure he had her phone number. That was a night she definitely looked forward to repeating soon.

"Where the hell were you?" Candi asked, her eyes wild. "I thought we had a plan."

Jessi stared at her roommate, still standing in the doorway. She had not been the only scantily clad woman making her way across campus after a night of fun. However, Jessi had not felt embarrassed or any shame over her actions. That was for boring girls. She was a slut and she took pride in her actions.

When the confusion on Jessi's face did not go away, Candi's tone softened. "I told you about the tailgating plan, didn't I?"

Jessi shook her head. "I don't even know what that is."

"It's the pregame party out in front of the stadium," Candi explained. "All the girls are going and we've got to get dressed up to show our school spirit."

"But the game isn't for hours," Jessi complained. "We've got time. Besides, isn't it all about being fashionably late."

Candi shook her head, partly enjoying the nonchalance her roommate had begun to demonstrate. And if Candi was honest with herself, she was a little jealous of Jessi. She had seen who she had paired off with. He had been hot. And since this was her first night away from the dorm, it meant it was a good one. And it was easy enough to read Jessi's expressions to know she had some morning sex. She was practically radiating with sexual energy. She was going to be a big hit tailgating.

Candi's night had been good, but not as good as Jessi's night. That was clear to her. Not that it mattered now. She needed to get Jessi ready for a full day of college partying.

"This is a group thing," Candi explained. "You'll understand what I mean soon enough. Now go get showered. I'll pick out your outfit for the day."

Jessi smiled as she grabbed her towel and kicked off her shoes, sliding her feet into a pair of sandals instead.

It was only when Jessi caught sight of her reflection in the bathroom mirror that she fully appreciated how her night had gone. Her makeup was messy, the eyeliner streaked, her lipstick spotty. Her hair was really what made it all look messy. Her hair stuck up at odd angles, like she had slept poorly. But it had been the sex. And if Jessi was honest with herself, she thought she looked really sexy. It was not how she wanted to go out and be seen by people, but her look screamed oversexed slut. It was perfect for the morning after a night like she had just had.

But now it was time to start her day afresh. Jessi showered and generally cleaned herself up. She dried her blonde hair and then put it up in a high ponytail. It gave her a youthful look that she liked. Then again, her makeup would help counterbalance that so she would not look too young. She was not a kid. She was a woman and wanted to look like a woman. She just also wanted to look like a sexy slut too.

When Jessi returned to her room, she found Candi already dressed to go out. She wore a Thatcher College t-shirt that had been strategically altered with large gashes and slices that revealed her braless tits underneath. Not that she was showing anything she should not be showing, but it was hot and slutty and made it clear that she held pride in her school.

There was a similar outfit laid out for Jessi. It sat on her made bed, not having had anyone sleep in it the night before. Although instead of rips and slices in the fabric, the t-shirt had been altered to more closely resemble a bikini top. Jessi and Candi had already altered several Thatcher College clothing items to make them sluttier, but this was new to Jessi. She had not seen it before.

"I bought a few extra items and spent the morning altering them," Candi said, answering Jessi's unspoken question. "Try it on."

And that was exactly what Jessi did. She dropped the towel that had covered her body, revealing her perfect nudeness before she started pulling on the top. Candi had a good eye for clothing and alterations. Part of Jessi wondered if

Candi would have been better off at design school. That was not the sort of thing Thatcher College had. Candi was certainly talented when it came to clothing alterations.

By the time Jessi and Candi left the dorms, Jessi looked ready to start a new day as a slut. Her tiny top placed the Thatcher College name right across her chest. The blue top did not show cleavage, but even Jessi's modest boobs could be seen a bit from the sides. The original t-shirt collar kept the top around her neck, but there was only a single tie that stretched around her back, just below the bottom swell of her boobs.

A thong and short denim skirt completed Jessi's look, along with a pair of high heels. It had only been a little over a week, but the only time Jessi had not worn heels since school started was on trips to the gym. This was not a gym day, however. This was a day for partying, drinking, and cheering on the Thatcher College football team as Cole took the field for the first game of the season.

"You're perfect," Candi finally said with a happy smile. "Now let's go meet up with the other girls and have some old college fun."

"I'm game," Jessi said, returning the smile. And she knew it would be a fun afternoon. The alcohol would be flowing and considering she had not eaten anything since dinner the night before, it was certain to hit her fast. Then she could get down to doing what she did best. Sex was fast becoming her favorite activity.

TAILGATING

"I heard you hooked up with Christof last night," Amy said with a big smile as she greeted Jessi with a hug. "Isn't he such a hunk? And he's hung like a stallion too."

"Oh yeah," Jessi said with a knowing look. She had to agree with Amy's assessment of her recent conquest. It had been a good night and a good morning, one that the tailgating plan had required to cut short. "He was fun."

"It looks like we're just going to have to top that today," Amy said, throwing her arms up in the air as they entered the stadium parking lot. "Woo," she called out, already excited for the first tailgating event of the year.

Jessi looked around and was surprised at how full the parking lot already was. The football game did not start for hours still, but there were already lots of people parked with tents going up and large grills heating up. She had no idea how big football was as a spectator sport. The whole event started hours before kickoff with a massive party in the stadium parking lot. And as hot sluts, Jessi and her friends were guaranteed welcome at almost every tent and grill around the place.

Amy took the lead. She was the most experienced of the crew when it came to tailgating at Thatcher College. Jessi had never been to a football game before, so she was as lost as could be. However, she was certain she would find her feet eventually, learning as she went. At the very least, she would be able to copy the actions of her friends until she found her own way.

They started with a tour of the parking lot, checking out who was set up and who was still a ways away from hosting anything fun. It was also important to be seen. Jessi might not have had the big tits like Candi, but she made up for it by showing off far more skin than the rest of the group. That had become her style, showing off as much bare skin as the situation allowed.

Deep down, Jessi knew her style had shifted immensely under the guidance of her roommate. Candi had pushed her to dress provocatively and in the short time since she had returned to campus with the goal of becoming one of the popular girls, she had taken that advice to an extreme. She definitely now had an in with that crew. She walked among them and even at times was looked at as a leader. However, Jessi was acutely aware that her fortunes could change. She could easily fall out of favor unless she kept pushing boundaries.

But as much as Jessi knew she had changed, she could not find one single thing she would give up from her new life. Sex was amazing and she was having lots of it. And as much as she was fixated on Cole, she was glad that she was getting to have experiences with many different men and even her roommate. That was something they were going to have to do again some time. Although Jessi had to admit her dance card was pretty full at the moment.

This weekend was a complete whirlwind for the newly minted hot slut and popular girl. The Friday night party and hook-up was only the beginning. The tailgating and football game were going to be fun. Then there were the Saturday night parties, where Jessi already had a dress picked out and she had invited a local girl to join them. And finally, there was an event with Professor Wright. Jessi did not know what to expect from that, but she was certain it would be worth it.

And all of those activities came before school started its second week Monday morning. It was not going to just be a rich and full day, but an entire weekend of fun and debauchery. Jessi could only imagine what the rest of the school year would be like. If this was an example of the fun she had missed out on in her first year at Thatcher, she was going to have the time of her life by the time the year came to an eventual close.

As Jessi and the rest of the girls made their way through the tailgating area, Jessi waved to a couple of the people she recognized. She saw Travis at one tent. Her mouth started to water the moment she spotted him. But it was not time to stop yet. They were still making their rounds, scoping out the situation before they started in on their fun. She even saw Jonas, which made her smile. He was her first fuck, but he definitely was not her last. But he had been good for a first time.

Jessi could hardly believe that experience had only been five days earlier. Considering what she had done since, the men she had been with, it seemed like a lifetime ago. She had finally begun her sexual awakening and she was making up for lost time. However, Jessi had no intentions of slowing down. This was who she wanted to be. It was unclear what that would mean long term, but considering she was still young, she decided not to worry about any of that. She was going to enjoy herself for as long as possible.

Finally, after finishing their first tour of the parking lot, Amy selected the first tent they should visit. It had been set up by one of the fraternities. There were a mix of current students as well as recent graduates. For the most part, all of the attendees were fit and strong, their bodies clear products of working out in the gym. And even after a bout of morning sex, Jessi was ready for some extracurricular fun.

"Welcome, ladies," one of the frat brothers said, welcoming the group to their tent. "Let me get you some drinks to start the day off."

Before Jessi knew what was happening, a cup of beer had been thrust into her hand. She happily took a sip. It tasted disgusting, but that did not stop her from drinking it. She never would have imagined that she would be drinking before noon, but that was what happened while tailgating sometimes. Not that she was going to complain. The whole weekend was for drinking, partying, and fucking. That was Jessi's plan.

Music started to play from one of the nearby vehicles and Jessi started dancing along to the beat as she kept drinking her beer. Candi soon joined her and the pair started bumping and grinding to the music, shutting out all other noises and ignoring the stares they got as the two sluts danced together. For the most part, Jessi kept her eyes closed, but when she did open them, she could not help but smile as she saw the attention she and Candi were getting.

In general, Jessi knew that was another thing that had changed for her. As Jessica, she had always strived to stay out of the limelight, all the while watching the popular girls with envy. Now she was one of those popular girls and she loved the attention she received when she dressed provocatively and showed off her sexuality for all to see. It was almost addicting and her mind was already working out how to attract even more attention.

"Thanks, boys," Amy eventually said after the crew had all finished their first drink of the day. The frat was only their first stop. They had other groups to meet with before kickoff.

Jessi followed her friends, a little disappointed that they moved on so quickly. The beer was hitting her, too, since she did not have any food in her stomach to slow the first effects of the alcohol. Not that Jessi minded. She had come to enjoy the buzzed sensations she got from drinking booze. It loosened her up and helped to make sure that any lingering remnants of Jessica remained hidden away.

But before she knew it, Jessi found herself with her friends at another tent. This one had drinks and food on the grill.

"Who wants a foot long?" the man behind the grill asked, jokingly.

However, Jessi and Candi both raised their hands immediately. It was only after a few moments that they both realized he was talking about food and not cocks. They giggled as they realized their mistake, but they did not for a moment care.

"How about you two share one?" the man offered. "I bet plenty of people would love to see that."

"Sure," Jessi said.

"Okay," Candi added.

Soon they were holding a foot-long sausage in a bun between them. They considered added condiments, but neither of them wanted to risk getting anything on their outfits. That would be poor form, especially so early in the day. It was better to hold off on such things for when there was no real risk of spilling.

With the foot long between them, Jessi and Candi started eating. They each bit off opposing tips and then worked their way toward the middle. Jessi had never eaten food like this or taken part in an eating contest. She swallowed as fast as she could, finding herself an even match for Candi. At least they had one thing they were even on. And when they reached the middle of the sausage, when their lips met, they paused their chewing and swallowing to share a kiss.

The hoots and hollers sounded off all around them. And it was not just the men who were watching and cheering them on. It was the women too. Amy let out a loud cry of support and other women, not all of them part of the hot slut crew, followed.

"That was hot," Candi said after they broke the kiss and she finished eating her half of the sausage. Jessi took a moment longer to recover, but she found it equally as hot. Her insides felt a bit like they were melting. Her fire, her arousal, was burning hot and driving her toward sex. She was not going to make it until game time without some sort of cock.

"You gonna lez out on us?" Amy asked, joking.

Jessi did not even react to Amy. Instead, she turned and grabbed the nearest man and laid a hot kiss on his lips. It only took a moment before the man responded, returning the sudden kiss and grabbing Jessi's ass as he did.

Moaning through the kiss, Jessi gently pulled her man of the moment toward a nearby vehicle. She was not sure if it was his or who it might belong to. She did not care. And it only took a moment before the man took the hint.

He opened the door and climbed in, scooting across the back seat. Jessi climbed in after him, closing the door behind her. However, Jessi did not sit down. Instead, she remained on her knees, leaning over the man's lap. She made quick work of his shorts, releasing his cock. It was already hard. It was not as big as some of the cocks she had experienced recently, but she was too horny to care about such things. She just needed that cock in her mouth. It was not a real foot long, but it would do the job.

The man groaned as Jessi started to bob her head in his

lap, taking his cock into her mouth and even letting it into the back of her throat. She had picked up a lot of tips and tricks since she first started sucking cock a week ago and she put all of them into action, making sure she got a dose of cum to accompany her half of the foot long she had just consumed. Skipping condiments meant she now got to use cum as a close addition to her sausage.

The man did not last long. Then again, that had been Jessi's plan. She had one thing on her mind. She wanted cock and she wanted cum. The man's pleasure was guaranteed, but she had needs too. Plus, she knew she had an audience. Even with the doors to the vehicle shut, she knew her friends were looking in on her, assessing her sluttiness. But it would not go unnoticed that she was the first of the crew to get a cock in her. She was not messing around when it came to being the hottest slut at Thatcher College.

Once Jessi had finally extricated herself from the vehicle, savoring the mouthful of cum she had received, she rejoined her friends. Another cup of beer was thrust into her hand and she drank from it happily, wanting to continue her fun.

And that was exactly what happened. Jessi, as it turned out, was not the only woman in the crew to get some pre-game cock, but she was the first and she made sure her friends all got to partake as well before she took part in a second round. However, before that could happen, the happily drunk Jessi found herself getting ushered into the game toward the student section to watch the opening game of the season. Jessi could not wait to cheer for her school, and especially Cole. But she also knew that if she did not get fucked during the halftime break, she would go a bit crazy. The blowjob had been good, but she needed to cum herself before long.

30

THE FOOTBALL GAME

Jessi had no idea what was happening. The game playing out in front of her made no sense. She knew Thatcher College was winning and she especially enjoyed watching Cole dominate on the field. He was like a fighting general, directing all of his teammates as they ran around on the field, at least while the team was playing offense. When the other team had the ball, Jessi lost most of her interest. Luckily, the other team never controlled the ball for long.

Looking up at the scoreboard, Jessi smiled to see her team up by a considerable margin. But more importantly, she enjoyed every moment of cheering for her team and her potential future boyfriend. Despite Cole wearing a helmet and pads, she recognized him easily on the field. There was only one player that he could be. Every time he had the ball, she squealed and screamed in support.

By the time halftime rolled around, Jessi was happy with the score and still very much drunk. However, she was surprised to find herself getting pulled out of the stadium by Amy and Candi, both of whom seemed much more familiar with football.

"Where are we going?" Jessi asked Candi, keeping her voice down so that only Candi could hear her question. As much as Jessi enjoyed her newfound role among the popular girls, she still wanted to make it seem like she was fully one of them. That meant not letting on when she was clueless. It was one thing to not understand football. There was a part of her that felt that was normal for a girl. But there was no excuse for not knowing how to be a proper hot slut in a situation like this one.

"Halftime means more drinking out in the parking lot," Candi said, smiling.

Before Jessi knew what she was doing, she was handed a shot glass by a handsome man. She downed it without even thinking about it, enjoying the burn of the alcohol as it went down her throat. A moment later, that same man took her by the hand and pulled her into a motorhome. Jessi did not protest. If anything, the events of her day thus far had been leading her to this point. She was horny and only a man's cock would fully satisfy her.

"That's it," Jessi practically screamed a minute later. Her skirt was pushed up around her waist and her thong panties were dangling around one ankle. She was on her hands and knees on the pullout bed, her current benefactor thrusting into her wet pussy from behind. "Harder. Fuck me harder."

In her short time as a hot slut, Jessi had found herself almost preferring rough sex. Sure, slow and sensual could be nice on occasion, but there was something about a hot and sweaty bang, a quick and hard fucking, that really got her motor going. She loved being on her hands and knees, her partner of the moment holding her by the hips as he slammed into her.

And her cried for him to fuck her harder did not fall on deaf ears. His pace quickened, heightening the moment for the both of them. And it only took minutes before he was filling her with his cum. Jessi screamed out as she shook with her latest orgasm. She honestly did not know how she could ever go more than a few hours now without getting herself off. And as Candi said, cock was always her first choice. Sex was more and more on her mind, giving her a goal to achieve.

Once it was all over, Jessi took a minute to put herself back together. She pulled her thong back on and then pulled her skirt down so that it actually covered her ass again. She ran her fingers through her hair, but was generally happy with her appearance. Stepping out of the motorhome, Jessi was greeted with a few of her friends. However, both Amy and Candi were both in a neighboring SUV, each of them getting railed from behind, just as Jessi had been moments earlier. Jessi might have been first, but she was not the last.

"Hey, do you want to do a keg stand?" someone asked.

Jessi turned to see another handsome man standing beside the one who had just fucked her. She had never bothered to get his name. It did not seem important. However, given her level of drunkenness, both from the alcohol she had already consumed and from the solid fucking she had just received, she smiled and nodded, not knowing what a keg stand was. But Jessi was willing to try just about anything in her current state.

This particular group of guys, belonging to one of the fraternities Jessi had yet to investigate, had brought a keg of beer with them. She followed the two men to a nearby tent where the keg had been placed. The men who were not busy fucking Jessi's friends were all there, red plastic cups filled with beer in their hands. They needed to drink fast if they wanted to make it back into the stadium for the second half kick-off, but Jessi did not know that. She had no idea how long halftime lasted.

"What do I do?" Jessi asked as she looked at the keg. Beer

was not really her drink, but she was willing to drink it to get the desired effect. That desire was to get drunk. Yes, she was already drunk, but she had discovered there were different levels of drunk and she could definitely get drunker.

The men explained what a keg stand was to Jessi. One of them even demonstrated, placing his hands on the keg handles and then let two others pick his feet up off the ground until he was doing a handstand on the keg.

"And I'm supposed to drink beer at the same time?" Jessi asked.

"That's how it works," the second man said. "You still game?"

Jessi did not need time to think over the decision. She was a definite yes. This new her was almost always up to try something new. Jessi smiled before she said, "Yes."

She placed her hands on the handles, just as the man had shown her. Then she waited as two men came around behind her and picked her up by the feet. Soon her blonde hair was falling around her face with her blood rushing into her head. A moment later the nozzle of the keg slipped between her lips.

"Ready, set, go," the man holding the nozzle between her lips said.

The beer started to flow and Jessi tried to drink it as fast as she could. It was made all the harder because she could not breathe, not even through her nose. But as the beer flowed and she sucked away, the men in the tent chanted out the count, keeping track of the time before she tapped out.

"10, 11, 12..." they counted as Jessi started to feel light headed. But still she kept drinking, not wanting to show any weakness in this new and admittedly fun activity.

"19, 20, 21..." Jessi was really starting to feel it. She needed to take a breath, but she wanted to keep going, not knowing how long she was supposed to last for. This was all new to her, but it was definitely fun.

"25," came the chant when Jessi finally tapped out. She could not go any longer.

The men hooted and hollered as Jessi was returned to her feet. She swayed for a moment, trying to find her balance in her heels. A little bit of beer dribbled down her chin. She grabbed a napkin off a nearby table and wiped herself clean.

"That was fun," Jessi said before she suddenly let out a loud burp. "Oopsie," she added, although no one seemed to mind. If anything, her new friends were impressed with her ability to go as long as she had. Jessi smiled, feeling like she finally belonged among the partying students of Thatcher College.

"Jessi, come on," Amy called out. "It's time to go back to our seats."

"Thanks for the beer and the fuck," Jessi said, waving to her latest friends. She might not know their names, but she was certain they would remember her for a while. She hurried off to rejoin the rest of the popular girls, mincing in her high heels.

"What were you doing?" Candi asked when Jessi returned to the group.

"I did a keg stand," Jessi said. She was happy with her results, but she could not avoid feeling overly full. Her stomach was not big enough to handle that volume of liquid. It was going to be a difficult few minutes before her body started to process all of that beer sloshing around inside of her.

However, if Jessi felt bad at all about her condition, she did not show it. If anything, she felt happy. It helped that she was generally a happy drunk. It was hard to get her down while she was intoxicated. But more importantly, she felt like she was really fitting in with her new friends, even pushing the boundaries as she went along. But more than that, she was finding herself more and more drawn to this lifestyle. The parties were fun, the slutty clothes were fun, and the sex was definitely fun. What more could a young woman like her want?

The girls were all impressed with Jessi's exploits, especially her lasting a full 25 seconds. Admittedly, the men who were counting might not have actually been counting seconds, but reaching 25 was still impressive in everyone's eyes. Jessi had gained further hot slut points with that performance.

"Hold it," said a security guard as the group approached the gate to go back in. "Have you girls been drinking?"

Given the way the whole group stumbled about, it should have been a rhetorical question. Of course they had been drinking. Pretty much everyone who reentered the stadium for the second half did so after imbibing. However, the guard was there to be on the lookout for those who drank too much, not wanting spectators to be too drunk.

It was unclear why Jessi suddenly did what she did next. It was not a conscious thought on her part. She just acted. She walked right up to the security guard and kissed him on the lips. She pushed her tongue into his mouth as her friends walked past him. He could taste the beer on her breath, but given the fact a hot blonde was making out with him, the security guard did not care. He let the girls go by him, without fulfilling his duty.

Just before releasing him from her kiss, Jessi snaked her long-nailed hand down toward his crotch and gave him the tiniest of squeezes. It was not meant to hurt him, but to tease him, to let him know that she was thinking about him in a sexual way.

The security guard could only stand and stare as Jessi swayed her hips back and forth, sashaying as she caught up with her friends. He seemed no longer to care about whether she and her friends had been drinking. And for Jessi, it was an important lesson. Sometimes it was better to turn off her brain completely and just act, to live in the moment, as well as the fact that sex could get her farther in life than using her brain. She would not have been able to talk her way out of the situation, but a simple kiss did the job for her.

Jessi's friends giggled as she caught up, complimenting her on her quick thinking, or lack thereof. And before she knew it, Jessi was back in her seat, just as the second half started.

It was another Thatcher College dominant half. Jessi screamed and cheered, especially whenever Cole was on the field. And those screams only got louder as the half wore on, her body processing all of that beer she had consumed at halftime. She got drunker and drunker and until she could barely stand up anymore. And yet she kept cheering her heart out, loving the fact that the home team kept rolling up the score. The game was not even close.

Afterwards, Jessi and her friends all stumbled out of the stadium. Jessi had wanted to run to Cole to congratulate him on a good game, but the players were all ushered under the stadium before her mind even managed to think about getting out onto the field. With the field clear, it was easier to just follow her friends.

By the time they had all exited and were back out in the parking lot, Jessi had one arm draped over Candi's shoulder and the other arm draped over Amy's shoulder. She used them for support, although the way they were swaying back and forth, it was clear they were drunk. Only now no one cared. Students filtered back toward the dorm rooms on the other side of campus. Alumni and other spectators returned to their cars and made the slow trip out of the parking lot.

"You're, like, my best friends ever," Jessi slurred. And she meant it. It had only been a little over a week, but she already felt a better connection with Amy and Candi than she had with anyone else in her previous life as Jessica.

Suddenly Jessi's phone buzzed and a jingle sounded out.

"Ooh, I got a text," Jessi said, stopping and fumbling for her phone. It was in the back pocket of her skirt. Somehow she had managed to avoid losing it during all of the extracurricular fun she had gotten up to earlier in the day.

The message swam in front of Jessi's eyes as she tried to focus on it. It did not help that she could not hold the phone completely steady. She was too drunk for this kind of thing, but she kept trying, eventually making out the message.

"It's Elsa," Jessi squealed happily. "She wants to join us at a party tonight."

Candi snatched the phone out of Jessi's hands. It was clear she was in no shape to answer. She could barely read, let alone type a return message.

"I'm telling her to meet us at eight," Candi said. "This should be fun."

"Now let's go get ready to party," Jessi said, charging off.

"It's this way," Amy said.

Jessi stopped and turned, suddenly realizing she had gotten turned around. Had she not been stopped by Amy, she would have ended up back at the stadium instead of at the dorms. Jessi giggled and then set off in the right direction this time. It was Saturday night and Jessi was certain she was going to have a fun night. She couldn't wait to add one more hot slut into the fold. And Jessi was certain she was going to get fucked again. Despite her halftime bang, she was aroused and wanting more.

THE NEW FRIEND

Elsa showed up at Candi and Jessi's dorm room a few minutes before eight. Both of the college sluts had been hard at work getting themselves ready for their night. Jessi had found a way to remain intoxicated, taking an occasional shot of vodka since returning from the football game. Jessi saw no reason to sober up before her night out. The fact was, she liked the feeling of intoxication.

Jessi was by no means a lush, at least not yet. And she did not feel a need to drink. However, as alcohol was relatively new to her still, she was continuing to experiment with it. She especially enjoyed how it seemed to keep any lingering doubts about her behavior away. The fact was, despite all she had done to change herself, Jessica was still there, just under the surface, waiting for a chance to escape and reassert herself. The alcohol made sure the inhibited Jessica remained dormant.

Even with her intoxication, Jessi had little trouble getting herself ready for the party. Her makeup was perfect and she was using a new pair of false eyelashes to make her eyes really pop. Even though this was her first time using them, they quickly grew on her and she made the decision to wear false lashes whenever it was feasible. They simply looked that good.

Jessi's dress was one she had purchased from the new shop Elsa was working at. It was pink, short, and featured various cutouts to display bare skin. The dress left almost nothing to the imagination and considering the placement of a few of the cutouts, this was not a dress to wear regular panties with. Even a thong or G-string would show through in some way.

Despite choosing to go commando the night before, Jessi decided to put her new C-string panties to the test. They were not made of normal material. The thing was plastic, designed to cover her pussy and reach up behind her and hold onto her body between her ass cheeks. If Jessi was honest with herself, the C-string was not very comfortable. A part of her would have preferred to go commando as she had done the night before, but she was committed to at least trying it for a night. It might grow on her.

Candi had also chosen to wear the clubbing dress she had bought Thursday at Elsa's store. Hers was lower cut to better display her tits, but it still covered more of her body. Her tits allowed her to do so much more and Jessi was definitely jealous of her roommate in that department. Jessi had not admitted it to herself fully yet, but she wanted tits like Candi's tits. She wanted them to be big and round and perfect. Her little bee stings simply did not measure up.

"Knock, knock," Elsa said as she slowly pushed open the dorm room door. It had been left ajar, making it unclear what Jessi and Candi's intentions were. The truth was, neither of them particularly cared if any of their section mates saw them getting ready for the party. It was a women's only section, so it was rare for men to wander the halls. Not that a man seeing them change clothes would have been a problem. If he was the right man, it might even mean he got a reward for his wandering.

"Elsa," Jessi squealed. Before Elsa had a chance to respond, Jessi wrapped her into a hug. "You made it."

Jessi's words and actions made it clear she was not sober. Not that Jessi cared. She had come to the conclusion that guys liked her more when she was at the very least tipsy. Her inhibitions were reduced and she was more naturally flirtatious. And if guys liked her more this way, then she would keep doing it. In a way, Jessi had become quite boy-crazy since returning for her sophomore year at Thatcher College. That had not been her intention, but she was enjoying herself enough not to care.

"Hi, Elsa," Candi said once Jessi had finally let go of their new friend.

"Thanks for the invite," Elsa said. "You have no idea how much I need a fun night right now. As you can probably guess, that job sucks, but I need it if I'm going to attend classes in the spring."

"You're gonna be a student here next semester?" Jessi asked, now even more excited than before.

"Yeah. I was supposed to start my first year this fall, but some funding fell through. But I made a deal with my family to come out here anyway and get a job until the funding gets squared away. I deferred my admittance until the spring semester."

"We're gonna be glad to have you," Candi said. "And hopefully you'll already have a friend group to join when you officially start."

"Normally I wouldn't have taken you up on the offer to join you," Elsa explained. "It would have just been weird. But since I'll already be a student here in the spring, I figured there wasn't any harm. And you're right. It will be nice to have friends from the start and not have to worry about being the new girl on campus when everyone has at least a few months to have made friends already."

"Um, but you probably shouldn't wear that to the party," Jessi commented, happy that Elsa was joining them, but not thrilled with her showing up in her work uniform. The hot sluts on campus had standards and none of them would be caught dead wearing black slacks and a blue polo like Elsa wore around campus, let alone to a party.

Elsa smiled as Jessi pointed out the obvious flaw in her outfit. The whole thing was all wrong.

"I didn't have time to change before leaving work," Elsa countered. "I just got off before coming here. But I used my employee discount to get a dress I hope is appropriate."

It was only then that Jessi realized Elsa had her hand over her shoulder with a hanger holding a dress in her hand. She had not caught on while she was hugging her new friend. The alcohol might have made Jessi less inhibited, but it also made her less observant as well. That was to be expected, but it left Jessi feeling a little strange, like she should have known better. Still, she was happy to see that Elsa had planned ahead and brought something to wear.

"You'll look awesome," Jessi said enthusiastically. "You can change in here if you want or I can show you to the bathroom to change there."

"I'm fine doing it in here," Elsa said as she pushed the dorm room door closed behind her. She might have been fine with letting her two new friends see her to change clothes, but she was not ready for complete strangers from the hallway seeing her that way.

It was only as Elsa removed her work clothes that both Jessi and Candi realized their new friend's potential. She was a hottie with sizable tits that had been hidden behind a restrictive sports bra and a nice ass that again, had been hidden beneath the poorly fitting work uniform. Elsa had some serious curves and with the right dress she would pull almost any guy she wanted.

And Jessi was certain that Elsa would do just that. While Elsa changed, she busied herself pouring shots for the three of them to get their night properly started. Jessi was already well on her way to an awesome night full of drunken partying and sex, but Candi and Elsa were both sober at the moment. That needed to change so she poured each of them a double while only pouring herself a single. They needed to catch up, even if there was no way they would manage to do so anytime soon.

"Wow, you look amazing," Candi said once Elsa slipped her feet into a pair of heels. Her baby blue dress was cut very similarly to Jessi's dress. Her friends already knew it, but Elsa was not wearing panties. Nor was she wearing a bra. The dress did not allow for that sort of thing without it looking extremely tacky.

"So hot," Jessi said, her voice slurring ever so slightly.

"Shots," Candi called out once she saw the row of shots lined up on Jessi's desk.

Despite all three women being under the age of 21, it was surprisingly easy to get someone of age to make a trip to the liquor store for bottles of booze. Jessi had never realized this fact when she was boring Jessica. Had she known that older students were perfectly willing to buy alcohol for their younger peers, she might have reached out to someone to explore that possibility. Now it seemed natural to her.

"You have no idea how much I need this drink right now," Elsa said as she picked up the double shot glass, filled to the brim with clear liquid. "I hate that job, but I only have to put up with it for a few months. Once the spring semester starts in January, I'm out of there."

"What should we drink to?" Candi asked, holding the other double shot glass.

"To being the best hot party sluts this school has ever seen," Jessi offered.

"Cheers," the other two women answered. All three clinked their glasses together before they quickly put their drinks away, swallowing quickly. Jessi let her shot flow down her throat, completely bypassing her taste buds. Vodka did not taste like much, but the alcohol still sucked. It was the inebriation that she enjoyed. She felt slightly out of control, which only enhanced her overall sense of happiness.

Elsa appeared less practiced with her drink, but it went down smoothly enough. It was also a double, which changed things. Candi, however, did not even wince when the alcohol went down her throat. She was a real pro about it. She was the reason Jessi had been able to make so much progress in becoming a hot party slut in such a short amount of time.

"I've got to fix my hair and makeup," Elsa said after putting down her glass. "Then I'll be ready to go. I'm excited. This will be my first college party."

"You'll be popular and have lots of fun," Candi said encouragingly. "You're definitely one of us."

Elsa nodded her head as she turned and used Jessi's mirror to put the finishing touches on her appearance. Jessi busied herself with pouring another round of shots while Candi texted Amy and the other girls about meeting up for the night's party. Or parties might have been the more appropriate term. There were several scheduled. Candi had already worked out the details. Jessi was too inebriated to notice and Amy had been focused on the football game. That had given Candi the chance to plan it all out.

When Elsa finished her work, she turned to let her

friends get a look at her improved appearance. Candi smiled, but Jessi stood there, staring, her jaw slack. She could barely believe the girl she had saved from the mall had turned into such a hottie so quickly. Clearly she was every bit a hot slut as the rest of them, even if she did not know it yet. Jessi had recognized her potential, but already Elsa was surpassing all expectations.

"You're so hot," Jessi finally said, breaking the silence. "I'm so jealous."

"Don't be jealous," Elsa said. "You're so much hotter than me. At least I think so. You probably pull in any guy you want."

Jessi had to admit that she did pretty well with the men on campus. It was just Cole who did not seem to want to fuck her yet. Everyone else was ready and willing. It was frustrating, but somehow she knew she needed to be at her absolute best before she could get with Cole. And even though he had no problem banging hot sluts, somehow once he chose her, things would be different.

"Amy and the girls will meet us at the first party," Candi announced, looking down at her phone and seeing Amy's text response.

"So another round then before we head out?" Elsa asked. She was only just starting to feel a slight buzz behind her eyes from the first double shot. She knew a second would probably take her past buzzed to drunk, especially drinking the two big shots so close together. But like Jessi, she did not care. This was going to be her first college party and she was going to make sure she enjoyed every moment of it.

"Cheers," the three girls said as they clinked glasses for a second time. They quickly drank down the vodka shots, slamming the glasses back onto the desk with satisfaction.

"Let's go," Jessi announced, almost leading the way out of the room. "It's time to do what girls like us do best."

"Party and drink?" Elsa said.

"And then get fucked good and hard," Jessi answered.

The three girls strutted and swayed as they left the dorm room. They were off to their first party of the night. How the night would end, none of them knew. But they were certain of one thing. They were going to have a lot of fun being the best hot sluts on campus.

PARTY IT UP

"Oh fuck," Jessi cried out as the cock pushed into her. She did not even know which of the three men was fucking her. Nor did she care. Jessi just wanted a cock in her pussy. And that was exactly what she was getting.

Three men.

Jessi already had one of them in my mouth. She sucked him off while Elsa busied herself licking her pussy. Candi was there, too, jacking off the other two men with her hands as they watched Elsa eat Jessi out.

She was such a dirty slut. She barely knew us and she was already getting involved in the fun. And her tongue felt divine as she had licked Jessi's pussy. She really knew how to use it.

There Jessi was, on her hands and knees. That was where she had been almost from the start. She had sucked that cock while on her hands and knees. That was where she had been when Elsa licked her pussy. That had been several orgasms on its own. Jessi prided herself in the fact she did not let those orgasms interrupt her blowjob. She could multitask when it came to cock.

Jessi looked on either side of her to see her two friends lined up beside her, one on either side. They too had cocks in their pussies. Or at least that was what it looked like from her vantage point. Although the strain on Candi's face made her wonder if she was getting cock in her backdoor. Jessi had not done that yet. She had never really considered it before. But even as she was in the middle of getting fucked by a big cock, she had started to think getting fucked in the ass was a matter of when, not if.

"Harder," Elsa called out as she bounced back against her man of the moment. "Fuck me harder."

She was already getting fucked hard, or so Jessi thought. And she wanted it even harder? Damn, Elsa was a bigger slut than Jessi had figured her for. And she was hotter. It had been impossible to know just how hot Elsa could be when she was wearing her ugly work uniform. But after seeing her in her tight party dress, as well as now with that dress striped off, she was far hotter than Jessi could imagine. How was she supposed to compete with that?

"Fuck my ass," Jessi suddenly called out. If Elsa was going to outdo her with her hotness, Jessi was going to have to go even sluttier. That was the only way to keep her place within the popular girl clique.

Jessi looked over her shoulder to see the man fucking her. She did not recognize him, but given his physique, she figured he was a football player. He deserved to celebrate after the big win. He gave Jessi a confused look for a moment, but then his mind seemed to kick into gear. He smirked, liking the idea of the slut he was fucking wanting him to fuck her ass.

Having nearly forgotten about the football game with all that had happened since then, Jessi's thoughts now turned to Cole. She was sure he was off fucking someone. She knew Amy was a frequent conquest of his, although it was simply a fuck buddy relationship. She knew Amy meant nothing to Cole. She was just a hot girl he could fuck. Jessi was hot, too, but not hot enough. She was not ready for him yet, whatever that meant.

Jessi found her heart sinking for the second time in as many minutes. However, all thoughts soon fled her mind and her moment of despair fled as the man's cock pressed at her tight hole. Her eyes opened wide as he slowly started to push inside of her backdoor, using her own juices and lubrication for his cock.

"Relax yourself," Jessi heard Candi say. It was little more than a whisper, almost sounding like a moan. Then again, with all three girls lined up next to each other, Candi did not need to speak loudly to be heard, even over Elsa's loud slutty moans.

Jessi took a deep breath and relaxed her body. That seemed to do it, because a moment later she felt the cock slip into her ass. He pushed into her, taking it slow. She bit her lip as she tried to figure out what this new sensation was. Getting fucked in the pussy had always felt good, like an overwhelming gush of pleasure washing over her. This was very different. But it was not bad.

Actually, as the man slowly pushed himself inside of her until she could feel his hips pressed up against her ass, a new sensation came over Jessi. She felt filled in a way she had never felt it before. Her body stretched, barely, around his cock, accepting him into her, but she had never felt so full before. It was new, it was different, and she liked it. Rather than the overwhelming pleasure she got from her pussy, this felt more like a slow burn of pleasure pulsing through her in time with her heart beat.

"Damn," the man groaned as he started to thrust in and out of her ass. It seemed like this was his first time fucking a woman's ass. Jessi certainly did not mind if this was his first time.

However, if Jessi was considering her situation, she would have been shocked at how short of a time it took her to reach this point. It had taken her just over a week to go from giving her first blowjob, to losing her virginity, to getting fucked in the ass. But there was no doubt in her mind that she was doing the right thing. She had never understood how good sex felt. She was glad to be rid of Jessica. Being Jessi was so much more fun. It felt better, too. And if she was lucky, she would manage to cum from her first ass fuck.

Elsa's loud moans continued to provide the symphony for the small orgy. Downstairs, the party was still in full swing. The loud bass line could be heard through the floor. It provided an additional rhythm to the already rhythmic fucking all three women received.

"I can't last anymore," Jessi's man called out. A moment later he unleashed his cum into her ass, filling her backdoor with his hot white seed.

But Jessi was cumming, too. This was different from her normal orgasms. It felt like a fire creeping through her body, but once it crested inside of her, she screamed out in orgasmic delight.

"Fuck, that's good," she moaned as the orgasm washed over her.

Candi and her man of the moment came a moment later. That left Elsa and his stud still to go. And there was no slowing down for those two. They paid the other orgasmic moments no mind as they kept right on at it. Elsa's ass got slapped as she got fucked from behind. Watching as she recovered from her orgasm, Jessi had to admire the slutty show Elsa put on. Yes, she might be trying to live up to the reputations of her new friends, but she was setting a high bar for the rest of them to meet going forward.

Finally the third set of fireworks went off. Elsa started cumming first, her whole body shaking as her orgasm shot through her. And that was followed a moment later by her man of the moment as he pushed into her one last time, emptying his balls deep into her pussy. They both eventually collapsed on top of each other in a sweaty and over-fucked heap.

"That was hot," Jessi finally commented as she watched her new friend slowly disentangle herself from her latest conquest.

And that was what these three men were. They were conquests. That was how she thought of it as a slut. Men were there to fuck them. It was just a matter of enticing them at the right moments to do it. Of course, the men likely thought of them as conquests. But that was what made a hot slut different from a normal woman. A normal woman did not think about men as objects to be conquered, to be fucked by.

As Jessi sat there, watching Elsa, a cock suddenly found its way in front of her face. It was only semi-hard, but she sucked it in between her lips. It was only after it started to harden again in her mouth that she flicked her eyes up to see that it belonged to the same man who had just been fucking her mouth. She shrugged her shoulders at what that meant, instead doing what a slut of her caliber would do, which was focus on the cock in her mouth and give it the best blowjob she was capable of.

Soon all three women were giving blowjobs, although Candi and Elsa switched partners. And all seemed to be going well. That was until the door to the bedroom opened. Jessi glanced toward the sound, wondering if the group was about to get yelled at by the party hosts. She had no idea who was hosting and they were clearly in someone's bedroom. Sometimes bedrooms needed taking over like his on a moment's notice, but it was not always welcome by the hosts.

However, rather than an angry host, three more men filed into the room. They, too, looked like football players, based on their builds. And as soon as the three new men had entered, the door closed behind them. The party just got a whole lot more interesting.

It was a proper orgy now, with the new participants. And Jessi was all for it. So were the other girls. Candi was the type of girl to never say no to a cock and it turned out that a drunk Elsa was similar. All three of them lost track of who they fucked or how many times they came. Even as one man recovered his stamina, there was always another cock ready to go. The three girls got fucked over and over again and they loved it.

When it was finally all over, when the party had run out of men to fuck the three happy sluts, Jessi took both Candi and Elsa by the hand and started the process of stumbling back to the dorms. Candi had finished the night by chugging a bottle of booze. She did not even know what it was. Her place of leadership over Jessi had been superseded by her drunkenness. Elsa was simply happy to follow along, a happy smile on her face from the multiple orgasms she had experienced. She had never partied like that before, but she liked it.

All three women had managed to find their dresses and their shoes, although Jessi had lost her C-string panties. She shrugged it off, deciding that they weren't that comfortable. It was better to just go without. It was easier, too, since she wanted to be ready to fuck at a moment's notice. At least when she was partying. It was a little different when she was wearing a short skirt to class. A nice pair of thong panties seemed to be right for that situation.

After two wrong turns, the three sluts managed to stumble back into the dorm. They were a giggling mess, but all three of them were happy with how their night went. Candi had gotten drunk and fucked to within an inch of her life. Elsa had blown off all the steam that had built up during her work the past couple days. And Jessi had fully accepted her new lot in life as a slut. She finally realized that this life was not just desirable, but what she was really meant for. There was no turning back.

Back in the dorm room, Candi simply collapsed onto her bed, passing out the moment her head hit the pillow. Elsa and Jessi were a little more with it, however.

"I can't drive home," Elsa said as she swayed back and forth and giggled at Candi's drunken state. "I'm still drunk."

"Then stay with me," Jessi offered as she started to strip off her clothes. She was tired and wanted to sleep, but she was not about to sleep in her new party dress.

Jessi had not meant anything specific by her offer, but Elsa started to follow Jessi's lead, taking off her dress. Soon the pair were both naked. And as Jessi climbed into her bed, Elsa followed. It was only when both women were safely tucked into the twin-sized bed that Jessi thought about the situation in a coherent manner. This was not what she had meant.

However, with Elsa's warm body, her soft skin, pressed against her, Jessi had a hard time finding a reason to kick her new friend out of the bed. And it was not like there was another bed for Elsa to sleep in. They might as well double up.

Not that Elsa was quite ready to go to sleep yet. Her hand moved up and gently traveled across Jessi's bare stomach, all hidden beneath the covers. Her fingers eventually found Jessi's small breast and gave it a little squeeze.

"Hmm," Elsa said. "I like your boobs."

Jessi did not know what to say, but pride swelled within her. Here she had been worried about Elsa. Her new friend had a hotter body and she was clearly a slut to begin with. She did not need training like Jessi did. However, Elsa also had shown an affinity for Jessi, both as a friend and as a lover. Elsa had already licked Jessi's pussy. She would not have done that unless she liked her.

"I like yours, too," Jessi said as she started to return the favor. A little light stroking and play before bed was just what she needed to help her wind down after taking part in her first ever orgy.

The two played with each other's bodies for half an hour, never making the other cum, but just enjoying themselves, before they fell asleep in each other's arms. Both of them had smiles on their faces. For Elsa, it had been a successful introduction to new friends who would help her fit in when she started school the next semester. For Jessi, it had been another sex filled day as she continued her transformation into her new and better self. She was still in her early stages, taking her first steps, but the foundation had been laid. She was just getting started.

3 3

MORNING AFTER

J essi woke up moaning. Her body felt better than good. Yes, there was a little bit of a hangover, mostly a headache that sat right behind her eyes, but that minor pain was easily ignored in the face of such overwhelming pleasure coming from her pussy. Jessi bit her lower lip as she reached up and started playing with her breasts. That further heightened the pleasure.

Although Jessi had no idea why she felt so good. Her mind was not working at full speed. It had not been working at full speed ever since the weekend started. Jessi had been either drunk or getting fucked. Those had been her two primary states and that had made for a great weekend. But that did not explain why she felt so good.

"You're such a slut," Candi said playfully.

Jessi turned and saw her roommate sitting up. She still wore her dress from the night before. She looked like she had been up late into the night getting fucked hard by a stud, or several studs. Then again, they all had.

It was only then that Jessi realized why she felt so good.

Elsa was between her legs, using her talented tongue on her pussy and clit.

Jessi lifted the blanket covering her to find Elsa between her legs, completely busy. For the briefest of moments, Elsa looked up, smiling, Jessi's juices trailing down her chin.

"Don't stop," Jessi moaned. Her hands kept playing with her small breasts, paying special attention to her nipples. They felt more sensitive than she could remember. Then again, she had never done much nipple play before. And with her pussy and clit taken care of by Elsa, it freed up her hands to explore other parts of her body.

Of course, Elsa had already returned to her work, her tongue lashing almost more than Jessi could handle. It was not the same as having a cock in her. It was different. But she was in no mood to compare the two. She simply did not want the pleasure flowing through her body to stop. If she could spend the rest of her life like this, feeling this good, nothing else would matter to her. It was as simple as that. The only thing that could make it better was if Cole was there. That was the one thing that was missing.

Jessi laid back and enjoyed herself. However, it did not take long for Candi to get in on the action. She pulled off her dress and retrieved her strap-on, taking little time to affix it around her hips. She then moved around to the foot of the bed, not far from where Elsa's plump ass pushed up from beneath the blanket. She needed to do very little to expose Elsa's pussy, just lifting the blanket up ever so slightly.

If it was not clear what Candi was doing, it became much more clear when Elsa's ministrations suddenly paused as Candi pushed the strap-on into Elsa's pussy. Jessi felt more than heard Elsa's pleasurable moan through her pussy lips. However, that pause was only momentary. As Candi started up a steady rhythm of thrusting into Elsa's pussy, Elsa resumed her tongue lashing, only this time it felt far more frantic. Not that frantic was a bad thing. It actually drove Jessi more and more wild.

"Oh fuck," Jessi cried out as she neared her climax. She wished she could wake up like this every morning.

"Look at these stupid sluts," Candi called out as she continued to hammer into Elsa. "All you can think about is sex."

Jessi found herself nodding her head to Candi's comment, agreeing without fully realizing what she meant. But it was true. At least it was true about the slut part and the part about thinking about sex a lot. It had only been a week, but Jessi sat there knowing she was addicted. There was no way she could go back to being Jessica anymore. That part of her life was truly over. Yes, she was still going to have to live with people thinking she was Jessica and not Jessi, but in time even that would pass. She was all Jessi now.

Elsa and Jessi came together. Candi could only smile as she watched the two sluts in front of her cum in near synchronicity. It had been a good call by Jessi to invite Elsa into the group. She was a perfect fit. She was hot and she was definitely a slut. And more than that, she was only a few months away from officially being a Thatcher College student too. The townie label, if she ever actually was given one, would soon be a thing of the past.

"Damn, that was good," Jessi said with a sigh as she sat back and relished the lingering pleasure that ricocheted through her body.

Elsa, however, was not satisfied. She followed Candi back to her bed and made quick work in removing the strap-on. A moment later, she had her head buried between Candi's legs, giving her the same treatment she had woken Jessi with.

Jessi turned and watched her friends play. She idly played with a nipple, keeping herself aroused. It was a Sunday morning and this felt like the perfect way to spend it. Sure, having a man or two around, preferably with big cocks attached, would have made the morning even sexier, but Jessi had no qualms with a sapphic morning. She had never been aware that she was into girls before this past week, but now it seemed like the most natural thing in the world. This was how life was supposed to be.

However, Jessi's relaxation was interrupted by the buzzing of her phone. It was a text message.

"Who is it?" Candi asked from her place on her bed. She was propped up on an elbow. Her other hand was on Elsa's head, guiding her movements. She was more particular about the way Elsa licked her pussy.

"It's a number I don't recognize," Jessi answered. She clicked on the message and started to read. "Looking forward to our rendezvous this afternoon. I'm using a burner phone to contact you. Only you have this number. If you're still deciding what you want to wear, I like school girls, the naughtier the better."

"I forgot about that," Candi said.

"Fuck me," Jessi exclaimed. "I did too. I was having so much fun this weekend I forgot I agreed to meet him today."

"Who?" Elsa managed to ask while coming up to catch her breath. Candi's guiding hand made it harder for her to breathe. Not that Elsa was complaining. She was enjoying herself, giving back to her new friends. And after all, Candi had been kind enough to fuck her to an orgasm. It was only fair that she repaid the favor.

"Jessi is meeting with one of her professors later," Candi answered. "They're coming to an agreement that should allow Jessi to live her best slut life without having to worry about school."

"Lucky," Elsa managed to say as she took another breath.

Jessi had barely thought about her deal with the professor in recent days. She had been too preoccupied with other activities. But the fact Elsa agreed that this was a lucky turn of events gave Jessi a little extra boost of confidence. She might not be the hottest girl on campus and she definitely was not the biggest slut, but she could hold her own. That counted for something. And Professor Wright obviously saw something in her or he would not have made the offer.

"I'm gonna go shower," Jessi said. "You girls have fun."

"We'll be here when you get back to help you get ready," Candi said before she broke out in a pleasurable moan.

Jessi simply smiled at the scene unfolding before her. She climbed to her feet, slipped her feet into a pair of high-heeled jelly sandals, a kind that worked well in the communal shower spaces. Then she wrapped a towel around her body and stepped out of the room.

The hallway was quiet. Jessi had no idea what time it was, but it seemed Sunday mornings were not a particularly active time in the dorms. It made sense. Students were sleeping off whatever debauchery they got up to the night before. Not that anyone else in the section could match the debauchery of Jessi, Candi, and Elsa. They probably ruled the roost in that department.

The hot water of the shower felt amazing, washing off the scent of stale beer and sex. Although the smell of sex was not all that stale. After Elsa's actions, it was fresh. Nonetheless, it felt good to clean herself up and start her day afresh. However, as she washed her body, Jessi was left with one thought. Her boobs were not big enough. Yes, she could be a slut and yes she could be called hot. But looking at Candi, at Amy, at Elsa, they all had bigger boobs. Unfortunately, there was little Jessi could do to match her friends at the moment.

By the time Jessi returned to her room, Candi and Elsa had finished their fun. Candi had managed to pull on a tight tank top and a pair of sweatpants, although the way she wore them kept up the sexy look. She looked recently fucked, which in a way she was. Elsa had only managed to put on the bra and panties she had worn the day before while at work. Jessi could tell she was not in the mood to put on her work uniform again. She did not blame her and would have chosen underwear to that if forced to choose.

Candi sat there smiling, like she knew something that Jessi did not.

"We picked out an outfit for you to wear," Elsa said, brimming with excitement. She bounced on her toes, making her boobs jiggle as an added benefit from her excitement.

Jessi turned to look at her bed and spotted the pink blouse and short tartan skirt. There were a pair of heels as well.

"The skirt is mine," Candi explained. "It should fit you fine. It's designed to fit different sizes. The blouse is yours, of course. So are the shoes. I just wish we had the right stockings to go with this. You'll have to buy some for next time."

Jessi nodded her head and dropped her towel. She was not bothered by Candi or Elsa seeing her nude. They already had and they would again in the future. Yes, they were both hotter than her, but they accepted her for being who she was. That was what mattered.

Jessi started with the skirt. It was shorter than she had first figured. She set the waist around her hips, letting it sit low. If she did not, the skirt would have ridden up, especially in the back, leaving her butt hanging out. That was not necessarily a bad thing, but she needed to get to the professor's house without causing a scene. It was best not to look like an oversexed student going to her professor's house to exchange sex for better grades, even if that was what she was doing.

But once Jessi had the skirt on, she had to admit it looked good on her. And since her friends had not set out panties for her to wear, she would once again go without. That was not something she had considered when all of this started. She had never guessed she would end up walking around half the time without panties. It certainly made sex easier, not having to deal with pulling a thong off or aside, depending on the moment.

The blouse followed. It was not designed to be buttoned up. There were no buttons, despite the fact there was no other way to fasten the two sides together, except by tying the two ends together. The material was thin, making it nearly transparent. The pink coloring was just dark enough to prevent her nipples from showing through, although that would not be possible if she were to get the top wet.

Jessi wore the dangling belly-button jewelry she had basically adopted from Candi. It had become her preferred jewelry and she wore it almost everywhere she went now. It was only the gym and a few other situations where she replaced it with another piece.

The heels completed the outfit. They left Jessi perched up high, making her legs appear even longer before they ultimately terminated beneath the tiny skirt. And they made Jessi sway her hips as she walked, allowing the pleated skirt to swish and sway as well, giving tantalizing glimpses of what might or might not be work underneath. Bending over was definitely out. Jessi would expose herself to anyone standing behind her. That is unless she wanted to expose herself. Professor Wright might like that.

Jessi had quickly become proficient at putting on makeup and styling her hair, but Candi and Elsa both joined in to help, helping to perfect Jessi's look for her professor rendezvous. She looked like even more of a slut when she was finished, yet there was a naïvety about her appearance that was hard to ignore. She looked every bit the naïve, but sexy, schoolgirl.

"You're ready," Candi announced at the end.

Jessi looked at her reflection in the mirror. Even she would never have guessed she could look like this when she made her decision. But she liked what she saw. She liked how she looked a little bit dumb. It was part of the naïvety she was playing up with her look. It left her looking like she might not really understand what was going on around her. And somehow, that was hotter than she could have imagined. Jessi felt herself growing wet already, just looking at her reflection.

"I'm ready," Jessi confirmed. "And I best be off. I don't want to be late to see Professor Wright."

Jessi threw on a long jacket that covered her outfit. It was too warm for the coat, but she wanted to keep her visit to her professor somewhat less scandalous, at least from an outside perspective. Once she was in his house, she planned to shed the coat and enjoy being his sexy schoolgirl.

Before Jessi left the room, she kissed both Candi and Elsa, giving them more than a little peck on the lips. It felt natural after what they had shared earlier in the morning. The kiss contained just enough tongue to make sure they were both a little turned on.

"Bye, girls," Jessi called out as she left the dorm room. Her heart pounded in her chest, but she could not wait to see how this latest adventure would work out.

A BATTLE FOR THE BODY

The campus remained sleepy throughout the first half of Sunday. In the past, Jessica would have already set up shop in the library, studying. Jessi, on the other hand, had no interest in the library. Who wanted to read books when they could meet with a professor for some direct tutoring? And given the heels and inability to spot her outfit beneath her long jacket, it was easy to guess what Jessi was really up to.

Not that there were many people paying attention to her as she crossed campus and then entered the adjacent neighborhood. Someday Jessi might have the confidence to do what she was doing without the attempted secrecy, but her first visit with Professor Wright was not that day.

The professor lived near campus. He was often spotted walking to and from campus. Not that Jessi paid that much attention. She just had the address and had picked out a route when she plugged that address into her phone. It was a relatively short walk, although it felt a bit longer given the height of her heels. Not that Jessi was complaining. They were a part of the outfit and she had come to enjoy the effect high heels had on her appearance. That was what mattered.

Jessi stopped and looked up at the house in front of her. The house number was the one Professor Wright had given her. And she had arrived right on time. This was not an appointment she wanted to be late for. When it came to parties, it was important to be fashionably late, but when meeting with the man who could make her hot slut life a million times easier, there was no way Jessi was willing to be late.

The house was a small bungalow. It was impossible to know if the professor owned it or was renting. But it was the kind of house that a single professor would live in. It was big enough to meet his needs without being overly ostentatious. He could probably afford more, but he did not need more. And with the beautiful Thatcher College campus so close and at his disposal, his needs were further simplified. But Jessi had no doubts that what she found inside would completely suit their needs.

However, this was a big step. Yes, she had already engaged in activity with the professor. She had sucked his cock in his office. That had been a positive experience and she would happily return to his office, even on a daily basis, if it meant she got to skip out on his classes and focus on the other areas of her life. But this was something else entirely. This was a step beyond what she had previously been thinking was reasonable or needed.

And yet, this was exactly what she had secretly believed her now friends were doing to keep their grades up before she met them. She always suspected they entered into these kinds of relationships, especially Amy, using their bodies to pass their classes. Jessi knew better now, but it was now her who was pushing those boundaries. And the truth of the matter was, despite this being a big step, Jessi felt good about it. This felt right. And she was excited to see what she could learn from Professor Wright and what benefits he could really bestow upon her.

Jessi was fully aware of what this moment meant for her. She had awoken something inside of her, especially in the last week, ever since that afternoon with Jonas. There was a fire that burned bright inside of her. That fire was lust. It drove her to want to be sex on heels. It made her feel good. It made her feel sexy. It made her horny, almost always aroused. And it made it so hard to think when she really got her motor going.

But just as Jessi was about to take her first step toward Professor Wright's house, her first step onto his front walk leading up to the front door, a wave of anxiety hit her in the gut. She nearly doubled over as the full realization hit her. She was about to fuck her professor so she did not have to worry about her classes anymore. She was giving up the knowledge she would gain by doing her schoolwork, by attending classes, by participating in her education.

"Stop it, Jessica," Jessi said to herself as she clutched at her belly.

That was what this was. It was Jessica fighting back. Jessi had thought she had banished her old self. After the weekend of debauchery that she had already put herself through, she thought she had killed off Jessica permanently. Jessica was a nobody. She was a boring nerd who no one cared about. Jessi, on the other hand, was popular. She had men practically lining up to have sex with her. She had friends, all of whom were sexy and slutty themselves. This was who she wanted to be.

Yet Jessica kept fighting back. The pain was almost more than Jessi could bear. And it was not just in her gut. It was in her head too, as if all of her drinking and partying had just returned to her with the biggest hangover she could imagine, a migraine that could level her for hours.

The world spun around her, her vision going fuzzy, but Jessi held on. Somehow she managed to keep her feet. She pushed back against Jessica, not letting her old self regain control. For that was what this was. It was a battle for her body, for her life. Jessi had been created by Jessica, wanting to be popular. But now that Jessi was in control, Jessica wanted back. She felt like two people, warring against each other for control of her body, for control of her life.

But who was in the right? Jessica had been there first, but she had created Jessi. She might not have understood how life would play out as Jessi, but she had done the heavy lifting all through the summer, getting herself fit and ready to become one of the popular girls. But now that she was clearly popular, Jessica wanted to rein her back in. Yes, it was possible to be sexy and smart. It was possible to be popular and a high achiever. But Jessi had found another possibility. She had discovered what it was to be a slut and she loved it.

"Fuck off," Jessi grunted. It was not particularly sexy or lady-like, but this was a war for her future. Jessica wanted to go spend the day in the library, studying. Jessi wanted to spend her afternoon in Professor Wright's house, doing whatever he wanted to do so that she could more easily enjoy herself. "You wanted this."

Jessica's hold on her body began to slip. It was true. She might not have understood what she wanted when all of this started, but she wanted this. She saw what it was to be sexy and popular, but only from the outside. Now that Jessi was both of those things, there were expectations as well as desires that could not be ignored.

And then there was the ever-present arousal. Jessi grabbed onto that and stoked the inner flames even hotter. Jessica recoiled at the heat, it being so unfamiliar to her in her past life. But Jessi was used to it. She reveled in it. The heat, the flames, the sex. That was who she was. That was who she wanted to be.

However, the final nail in Jessica's coffin, at least for the time being, was Cole. Jessica was just as enamored with Cole as Jessi was. That was something they shared. But Jessi knew this was the life she needed to live to get with Cole. They had a future together. She had no idea how long their relationship would last. Maybe it would not survive past their time at Thatcher College. But that was the relationship they both wanted. And the only way to get to that point was through Professor Wright.

That was the final straw. Jessica retreated. She was not gone, but she was beaten. The pain cleared. Jessi stood upright again. She looked around her. The street was empty. No one had just seen her struggle. At least no one out on the street had seen it. Someone could have spotted her out a window. Even Professor Wright could have if he was looking for her. But she could not worry about that. She had an appointment to keep.

As Jessi stepped forward, she could barely think straight. Her fight with her past self had left her turned on almost as much as she usually found herself after spending an hour with Cole. If Professor Wright did not fuck her, she did not know what she would do. But her arousal did mean one thing that would probably ingratiate herself with him even more. There was absolutely nothing she would say no to. Any desire of his she would fulfill, as long as she saw a chance to cum. It was as simple as that.

Climbing the steps to the front door, Jessi felt the heat of her body more than ever. She wanted desperately to throw off her jacket, fully embracing the sexy schoolgirl that she had dressed as. With Jessica in retreat, she wanted to further put a stamp on her life, adding ownership that would be nearly impossible to ignore. Even if Jessica managed to regain control in the future, it would be too late. Everyone would know her as Jessi, the hot and sexy slut. She would have to live with that forever.

Yet, Jessi managed to hold off. It was not just her reputation that mattered in this case, but also Professor Wright's reputation. What they were about to engage in was considered taboo, at least from the standpoint of campus administration. If the professor was not tenured, he could lose his job for doing something like this. And given his age, it seemed unlikely that he had been granted tenure yet. Therefore, Jessi needed to hold back and not expose her true intentions. At least, not yet.

Jessi took a deep breath, trying to steel herself for what was about to happen. Even as Jessi, with all of her heightened arousal, she knew this was a big step. It was a step that could not be walked back. But she was certain this was the right move. It was what she wanted.

The sound of the door bell could be heard as soon as Jessi pressed it. It was muted, having to pass through the door, but it was there. The sound was followed by footsteps on hardwood floors. She could hear them. Then the door opened. There was no turning back. It was on.

PUNISHMENT

The front door opened. Jessi looked up to find herself looking into Professor Wright's eyes. He looked her up and down, his eyes taking in her bare legs and high heels. Seeing this, Jessi opened her jacket. She pulled it apart to reveal the rest of her slutty schoolgirl outfit. His eyes lit up, seeing how she followed through with his instructions.

The professor stepped back and held the door open for his young protege. He said nothing as she stepped into his house. And as soon as she was inside, her eyes scanned the entryway. The house looked as she had expected it to look. Jessica had visited professor's houses before, although not in this capacity. Some professors were known for holding backyard parties for the final class of the semester. Or indoor parties, since the end of the fall semester fell in December when it was too cold and dark to spend that time outside.

But obviously this was different. Professor Wright lived in a small bungalow. His furniture was tasteful and expensive enough that Jessi reminded herself that this was not a college party. She should avoid spilling drinks and she should generally be wary of causing damage. However, the hardwood floors and general appearance of the house made Jessi feel welcomed. She doubted anything bad could happen to her here.

"You're late," Professor Wright growled, his first words since Jessi arrived.

In reality, Jessi was only about two minutes late. She had spent that time out on the sidewalk, battling herself on whether she should make her visit or not. Jessi had won the battle, but now she sensed that there would be retribution for needing to have the battle in the first place. It was all the more reason to dislike the woman she had been and embrace her new self.

"I'm sorry, professor," Jessi said. She had no idea that Professor Wright had seen it all. He knew she struggled with the idea of paying him this visit. But now that she had entered his home, he was going to make sure that she understood the power dynamics at play between them.

"You're not yet, but you will be soon."

Jessi shrugged off her jacket to better expose her body to her professor. His eyes trailed up and down front, pausing on her bare midriff and the pink jewelry in her belly-button. She did not have the chest to automatically draw a man's attention, but her tight midriff, along with the accompanying jewelry, certainly helped make up for that fact.

"Have I been naughty?" Her voice was sensual and filled the air with sexual tension. She knew her part in all of this. Yes, she was the submissive schoolgirl, but she was also a seductress. She wanted this as much as Professor Wright wanted it. She might have even wanted it more. She certainly wanted what he was offering in exchange for this game. The ability to slack off in her studies while keeping her grades up was an important part of her future at Thatcher College.

The professor's eyes lit up with a fire and lust at the word naughty. Jessi had never seen that response from a man before. Despite her whirlwind tour of being a slut over the past week, she still remained woefully ignorant of so much in the world of sex. Yes, she loved the hot and hard sex with well-hung college men, but Professor Wright was an entirely different animal. Yes, he was well hung as well, as she already knew, but he had far more experience than even she understood. And she was about to face that head on.

Professor Wright played nice to start. He took Jessi's jacket and hung it up on a hook by the door. He kept the front door unlocked. He had no need to keep Jessi trapped inside his house. Yes, she had ignited his darker impulses, but he had confidence she would stay and that this meeting would be the first of many. However, should she become overwhelmed by the demands he placed on her, the door would remain open, giving her the opportunity to leave. He felt no need to punish her outside of the house, only inside.

"Naughty enough for a punishment." The professor took Jessi by the hand and pulled her into the living room. He sat down on the couch and pulled her down on top of him.

Jessi let out a squeal of shock as she suddenly found herself bent over her professor's knee. Her skirt rode up, revealing her lack of panties. She had not entirely been sure what Professor Wright had planned for them, but she expected she would be sucking his cock and letting him fuck her. But this was far more than she had imagined.

And yet, despite this being more than she expected, she did not recoil at his touch. In fact, she squirmed as he ran his hand over her bare ass. Her pussy dripped in anticipation, not knowing exactly was about to befall her, but enjoying it nonetheless.

"I think I'll start small. Four spankings for each minute you were late. You were two minutes late, so that means eight in total. Does that sound right to you?"

Jessi bit her lower lip as she continued to squirm. This

was an entirely new experience for her and she did not know how to respond. And yet, she felt completely helpless as she laid there, her ass presented to her professor, his hand running across her bare skin, caressing her sensitive bottom.

"Answer me," he demanded, his other hand grabbing Jessi by the hair and pulling back.

Pain flashed through Jessi's scalp, but it wasn't a hard pull. It was just that she had not been expecting it. And, if anything, the small bit of pain made her all the wetter, all the more aroused.

"Yes, sir," Jessi called out, her voice strained, laced with need. She needed to cum. Her body had already been turned on. That seemed to have been a result of winning the battle against Jessica. But now she was horny and desperate to cum. She did not know how long she could last before her arousal drove her crazy. She might end up humping the furniture to seek relief.

"Professor. Yes, Professor."

It was a simple command, but already Jessi was starting to understand. She was to call him Professor. That was, after all, his title. And it had become more and more clear that she was here for tutoring. It was just going to be a very different sort of tutoring than she had first expected. Yes, sex was surely going to be on the table, but first, her professor had a few other activities he wanted to put her through.

"Yes, Professor," Jessi repeated. Already, her second lesson had been learned. She already knew not to be late. Now she knew how to address him. And luckily, using his title in these situations would not lead to suspicion when they were on campus. It was entirely normal for her to call him professor in class and when they saw each other elsewhere on campus. No one would suspect the extracurricular relationship they had.

"Now, I want you to count each spanking and thank me. Can you do that?"

Despite Professor Wright's stern actions, there was a kindness in his voice. Yes, he was punishing her, working out a certain degree of anger, but it was clear that he was also teaching her. He was teaching her how she should behave with him. And Jessi absorbed this new information like a sponge. She was certain not to disappoint him again in the future.

"Yes, Professor."

"Good. Now we can begin."

The first slap came down on Jessi's right ass cheek. She yelped as pain flashed through her body, followed by a steady throb.

"One," she called out. "Thank you, Professor."

His open hand came down against her ass again, this time targeting her left ass cheek.

"Two. Thank you, Professor."

He went back and forth, alternating and only pausing to give Jessi the chance to give him the count and thank him for her punishment. For Jessi, her punishment felt as if it lasted half an hour. For Professor Wright, he felt as if he was just getting warmed up. Then again, it had been a long time since he had someone like Jessi in his lap. He wanted so much more, but he knew he had to work up to it. He had not even spanked her that hard. Future punishments would likely bring tears to her eyes, in addition to a red and sore bottom.

"What have you learned?" Professor Wright asked.

"I learned not to be late to our tutoring sessions, Professor," Jessi answered. She turned and looked up at him. Her cheeks were red to match her bottom, but there was also arousal in her eyes.

The professor smiled as he looked down on his protege. He was already imagining the fun they could eventually have together. He had a whole closet full of toys he hoped to one day use with her. But that would all have to wait. For now, it was a simple matter of making Jessi comfortable in their new relationship. Professor Wright had no delusions that this would become a proper relationship. It was sex. It was sex in exchange for him not only giving her good grades in his class, but him persuading her other professors to cut her some slack, if not giving her the same basic deal as he had, although he figured her other professors would not get to sample her sexual skills like he would.

"You're very wet down here," Professor Wright mentioned as he slid his hand from her reddened ass to the junction between her legs. Her bare pussy was almost to the point it was leaking onto his pants. Luckily, he planned to do laundry after she left, but it was good to know in advance just how wet and horny Jessi could get.

"Yes, Professor."

Jessi squirmed more as he fondled her pussy lips. However, it was not in an effort to get away. No, she liked how he touched her. She wanted more of that. She needed more of that. Her arousal was already beginning to cloud her mind. She went into a similar headspace as she did when she was with Cole. The only difference was Professor Wright was unlikely to leave her hanging. Even if he did not fuck her, she seemed certain to cum.

"Just horny bitch in heat, aren't you?"

"Yes, Professor," Jessi agreed. She was at the point she would agree to almost anything he said. Yes, she still had a voice inside of her that could bring her down from the edge if they went too far, but nothing they had done came anywhere close to Jessi's red lines. Despite her punishment, she was still very much enjoying herself. And there was still the important prize of what this relationship could do for her grades. It was hard being a hot slut and a good student. This way she could be both without issue.

"I like that," Professor Wright said. "And I know just what to do now. I want to keep you right on the edge while you keep my cock warm."

Before Jessi even realized what was happening, she found herself kneeling on the floor between her professor's legs. She sat back on her heels, not bothered by the lingering soreness from her earlier punishment. Then his cock was out and Jessi found her mouth watering.

"Here's how this is going to work. Your job is to keep my cock hard. I'll cum when I want to, not when you want me to. Understand?"

"Yes, Professor," Jessi answered, although she was not entirely sure on how this was going to work. Still, she was going to do her best. It was not the sex that she craved, but it was better than nothing.

"And while you act like a sleeve for my cock, I want you to play with your pussy. But you aren't allowed to cum until I do."

Jessi wanted to scream in frustration. She already felt as if she was on a knife's edge. How much more stimulation could she handle before she came? And she wanted to cum. Her whole body felt primed, now more so than ever after the spanking she had received. But she would do her best to fulfill Professor Wright's requests of her. That was why she was here. She understood what the stakes were and she was more than up for them.

"Yes, Professor," Jessi said, nodding her head.

"Then begin."

And just like that, Jessi found her mouth filled with cock as her fingers worked deftly to tease her pussy. His cock hardened in her mouth, even more so than it already was. It seemed the professor enjoyed her punishment as much as she did. However, she did not let herself push him over the edge. She held back, not knowing when she would get his tasty treat, if at all.

But the final piece of the situation came to life when the professor turned on the television. The sound of a football game filled the room. Jessi could not see the screen from her position. It was directly behind her and she could not let the professor's cock out of her mouth. However, she did glance up and saw that Professor Wright's eyes were on the screen, watching the game. He was not paying attention to her. She was merely a flesh-light, an object to keep his cock wet and hard. And somehow, that was hotter than anything.

PROFESSOR WRIGHT'S GOALS

Jessi felt like her mind was broken. She had Professor Wright's cock in her mouth and her fingers were busy diddling her clit. She had not cum. Every time she got close, she backed off just enough so that she could recover, only to start diddling herself all over again when she could handle it.

Actually, that was not dissimilar to her cock sucking work. Acting merely as a cock sleeve, her goal was to keep her professor's cock in a semi-hard state, never letting him get too close to the edge himself. And when she sensed that he was starting to get close, she backed off, trying to go as still as possible while keeping his cock in her mouth. And all the while, Professor Wright kept his attention on the television and the football game playing.

Jessi had only ever watched one football game in her life. It had only come the day before, but she had been too drunk to really understand the game. She just knew when it was time to cheer. She had been able to marvel at Cole's athleticism, his strength, and his skill, but she did not understand the game any better for that. However, that game had felt like it was in her long ago past. So much had happened since then and her mind was not exactly working at full speed at the moment.

The constant edging made it hard for Jessi to think in her current state. The arousal made her want to jump up and ride her professor hard. She needed his cock in her pussy. She even would have accepted it in her ass, although she was still a bit sore back there from the night before. All she knew was she was desperate to cum. She needed an orgasm like a fish needs water. She had no idea how much longer she could last.

But it was not just that Jessi's mind felt broken. She had internalized the instructions she had been given and her body acted on those instructions instinctually. There was little to no thinking involved. Had Jessi been able to process this fact, she would have enjoyed it more. There was a certain joy in not having to think. All she had to do was what she had been told, letting her body take care of the rest. And that was exactly what she did. No thinking, just action.

"Fuck," Professor Wright said. Jessi was unclear if he was reacting to the game or if it was related to her ministrations. Her brain processing power had been reduced to such a degree that she could not fully register the meaning behind his single utterance.

However, a moment after the sudden comment, Professor Wright reached over and picked up the television remote. Then silence filled the air. Jessi did not know if the television had been turned off or if it had just been muted. She was not about to turn her head to look. That would have meant taking the cock out of her mouth and that was against the rules. Jessi had already been punished once and she did not want to let that happen again.

"You make a great cock sleeve."

Jessi inwardly beamed, loving the compliment. Of course,

it would have been a strange compliment had it been given to Jessica. But as Jessi, with her mind blissfully blank, she could only take it as a compliment. Right now, she was little more than a sexual toy, barely a person, at least in mind. Her body, however, was definitely real. She was tight and available, in more ways than one.

Not that getting complimented as a cock sleeve took away from the work she was being complimented for. She continued just as before, unwilling to do anything else until Professor Wright commanded her. For that was why she was here. She was here to do what he wanted, to play out whatever fantasies he might have. She was his willing plaything in exchange for a lightening of her academic load. It was a simple trade of grades for sex.

"Stand up for me."

There was a part of Jessi that wanted to continue her current work. The truth was, even though her jaw was getting tired, she liked having a cock in her mouth. She liked being kept on the edge of orgasm. She liked the blissful mindlessness that had filled her head.

However, there was no way she could refuse her professor's command. She released his cock from between her lips and dropped her hands away from her pussy. Then she carefully rose to her feet. But her arousal was evident. Her eyes, which appeared mostly vacant due to her current state of mind, remained locked on Professor Wright's cock. She kept her head bowed, just so that she could continue to look upon his manhood.

Using a moment to take her in, Professor Wright noticed how she seemed to sway slightly, her body tired from kneeling before him, sucking on his cock as slowly as possible, for the better part of two hours. He already sensed that her mind was not in the same state as before. Her balance was slightly off. Some of that was surely her heels, but she had managed to remain surprisingly still for a long time.

Regardless, he doubted Jessi had any sense of time. She was too hot, too horny, to even understand time at the moment. If he could somehow manage to keep her in this state permanently, he would have a bimbo sex doll all to himself. He had heard rumors of other professors taking students like Jessi in. Once it became clear they were not really college material, it was easy to push them into their new lives. With a little guidance, they did it willingly.

Jessi was a different case, however. Professor Wright had done some checking up on her. And the student who stood before him now, fixated on his cock, was not the same student who had made her impression on the professors during her freshman year. Now a sophomore, Jessica had changed, becoming Jessi. It was a miraculous transformation. She had gone from nerd to hardened slut over the course of the summer and he was all for it. He wished more women made that transition. He liked having the eye candy in his classes.

Since Jessi had a past as a top student, he enjoyed seeing her like this even more. Sure, there were ways she could have been hotter. Her chest was lacking, although her butt looked pretty good in her little skirt. The blonde hair and midriff-baring tops really fit her slut look and Professor Wright fully approved. Then again, he had a thing for bare midriffs, especially when they were decorated with belly-button piercings like hers was.

However, knowing Jessi's past gave Professor Wright pause with how he wanted to continue this mutually benefi-cial relationship. Unlike some of those other female students who were forced to get by academically through the use of their bodies, Jessi could always go back to being her old studious and nerdy self. Yes, she clearly wanted this, at least to some degree, but he could not push her too hard. Rather than break, she would revert and there was no way he wanted that to happen.

Jessi reverting to Jessica would mean not only that the school and the world would be missing another hot slut, but that she might feel the need to tarnish his reputation. Professor Wright was tenure tracked, but he had not yet achieved full tenure, meaning the college could fire him for almost any reason they determined as cause. He liked his job too much to risk that. Therefore, he needed to bring Jessi along slowly. He needed to be careful.

The fact Jessi had accepted his punishment for being a couple minutes late had been a good sign. She was willing and even interested in this relationship. Not that his reasons for punishing her were particularly strong. He had watched her outside from the window, easterly anticipating her visit. He had seen the struggle she showed as she stood in front of his house, trying to decide what to do. And it was clear that she had chosen this, because she would not be standing before him otherwise.

"The first time I fuck you, I want to do it here," Professor Wright explained. "This is the place where you were punished and where you served me. But I also want to make this a place of pleasure. In the future, we will likely fuck in other rooms, moving eventually to the bedroom if you continue to be a good slut for me. Do you understand?"

He had no idea if Jessi was in a state where she could understand him. Her glassy eyes made it clear she was not doing a whole lot of thinking at the moment. Actually, if the professor admitted it to himself, he found the whole idea of her being a bimbo to be hotter than anything else he could imagine for her. Except unlike the other bimbos who somehow made it into Thatcher College, she would have chosen this life for herself. She would have dumbed herself down willingly to make it happen.

Finally Jessi nodded her head. "Yes, Professor," she added, her voice barely a whisper.

Any other time, he would have asked her to speak up, but he did not want to break her out of the arousal trance she was now in. He liked her this way and hoped she would eventually come to associate her time in his house with the mindlessness she now expressed. She had been sexy already, but the vacant expression sent her over the top.

Jessi was not fully aware of herself. She understood what she had just agreed to, but the prospect of eventually fucking in his bed seemed like a far off proposition. It was too far into the future for her to even consider at the moment. Instead, however, she was focused on getting the professor's hard cock in her pussy. She needed it more than she could possibly imagine. And she would do anything he asked just so he would fuck her. She was his to command.

"Come sit on my lap," he beckoned.

Jessi smiled and turned. She then lowered herself down onto him slowly. Professor Wright grabbed her hips and guided her down, lining her up with his cock, which was hard and ready for the main event. He had never had someone keep his cock warm and hard for that long, but he was definitely ready to fuck now. He might have been tempted to keep going, but his team was losing badly and there seemed no hope of a comeback. It was far more enjoyable to fuck now, although he hoped he could train Jessi to last for an entire game in the future.

The moment Professor Wight's cock pushed up into Jessi's pussy, she let out a long low moan. Her body shuddered as a wave of pleasure shot through her. She was already so turned on that the increasing pleasure was actually a relief. Even though she remained far from orgasm, her body knew that having a cock inside of her meant an orgasm was imminent.

The professor guided her hips down until she had taken all of his length inside of her. She was wetter than any woman he had ever been with, although her pussy was still tight, almost fitting his cock like a glove. Professor Wright had bedded enough women in his life to get an idea of what he liked and he had never found a pussy he liked more than Jessi's.

Jessi did not move once she was fully seated. After all, she had been commanded to sit on his lap. Getting his cock in her was just a bonus. And it was a good thing she had not been wearing panties, because they would have just gotten in the way. If she was honest with herself, her days of wearing panties, unless needed, were mostly over. Although there were different reasons she might need to wear them. It would not do to have her juices running down her legs when she was too turned on while in public.

Finally, however, Professor Wright started to guide her into proper movements. And once freed to fuck properly, Jessi started to bounce and grind on his lap, fully enjoying the moment of being filled with her professor's cock. It felt good. It felt better than good. It felt right. The only thing she could imagine feeling better was when Cole finally fucked her. That remained her top goal.

Once Jessi started moving on her own, that freed the professor's hands to move away from her hips and to start enjoying other parts of her body. She still wore her skirt, but it was pushed up around her hips, having been barely long enough to cover herself before. But it was Jessi's top that he gave special attention to. He rubbed her small breasts through her thin pink blouse, causing Jessi to again moan as she now had another point of pleasure flowing through her body, filling her mind with a fog of arousal.

But the professor was not content to just cop a feel through her blouse. Luckily, his fingers were more than nimble enough to untie her blouse. Soon her chest was fully exposed and the professor's hands kneaded her breasts as she continued to fuck him as best she could.

Jessi threw her head back and closed her eyes and she reveled in the pleasure. After the past almost two hours, she was more than ready for a proper cock to fuck, but more than that, her body was primed to accept all the pleasure she could get. All that hard work was finally paying off, delayed gratification of the most delicious sort.

When Professor Wright finally came, his cock surging with his hot white seed inside of her, Jessi came too. Their bodies were an example of synchronous perfection, cumming together. Jessi screamed out as she came, massive waves of orgasmic pleasure erupting inside of her. The cascading pleasure flowed through her body, reaching every inch, from her toes all the way up to the top of her head.

Jessi's mind went completely blank as all her thoughts and feelings of the moment were obliterated by the over-whelming pleasure. She had never cum like this before. It was better than she could have expected. The past few days had been one long fuckfest, but this put the final cherry on top of the sex sundae that had been the first full weekend as a proper hot slut. And even if Jessi could not think or even really feel beyond the overwhelming pleasure, there was no doubt in her mind that there was no going back.

Jessica might try to reappear in the future, but given the incredible pleasure she just received at the hands of her professor, Jessica would always struggle in winning the argument for supremacy. How could Jessica deny Jessi that kind of pleasure? It was like a drug, one that she would soon become addicted to if she was not already.

And when it was all over, Jessi found herself putting on

her jacket to return to her dorm room. Her hair was messy, somehow having gotten that way in her multi-hour visit. If anyone asked what had happened, she knew she would say that she was receiving tutoring from her professor, but it was hard to believe anyone would believe that. Next time, she would need to bring a bag with hair and makeup products so she could repair the damage of their sexual escapades.

There was no doubt there would be a next time. Professor Wright all but told her to return next week at the same time. And she would. Jessi had loved her Sunday afternoon of tutoring. It had been a great time, especially if he kept her cumming like that. It was so good she could almost imagine herself losing interest in Cole. Almost. The star quarterback remained her primary target, but if that somehow did not work out, bagging a professor would be a good consolation prize.

In the meantime, Jessi was going to enjoy not needing to think much about her classes. Professor Wright promised to talk to her professors and get her out of any future work. He could not promise her she would ace her classes, but as long as she was passing, she was happy. Sure, her chances of graduating with honors at the end of her four years seemed unlikely, but all this sex was worth more than an honors designation on her diploma.

However, Jessi still had no idea what this new academic-free life would be like. Her past week had awakened a sexual creature she never knew existed within her. Now, for the first time, she was able to let it loose without fear of repercussions. But many questions still remained. But as Jessi walked back to campus, she was in no mood to look for answers. She was just going to enjoy the post-orgasmic glow for as long as possible.

NEVER ENDING

By the time Jessi returned to her dorm room, Elsa was gone. Her night of fun was over. She needed to return to the mall to work another shift.

Jessi felt bad for her new friend. Elsa did not have the freedom that college afforded the rest of the hot sluts. It was then that Jessi realized how truly lucky she was. The expectations for her were limited, since all she was supposed to be doing was getting an education. Or, more accurately, Jessi was supposed to be getting good grades. And now she had solved that problem. She had to hope Professor Wright's intervention on her behalf would free her up even more.

Not that Jessi felt compelled to skip classes. It was just that she no longer felt the need to pay attention. Her reason for going to class was to meet cute guys. She was a slut on the prowl now, always. And it felt so good. She loved the constant sex. She had no idea how she had never been with a man before this new adventure began. Sure, Jessi had masturbated on occasion, but this past week had awoken something inside of her that she never knew existed before.

Jessica had solely been interested in academics. At least that was what it felt like now that Jessi looked back on her past life. Obviously there had been the desire to be popular, but Jessica had no idea what being popular really meant. Luckily, the work she had done over the summer had set her up well to be Jessi.

And the guidance from Candi had been immeasurable. Jessi did not know what she would have done without her. How she had been so lucky to be assigned such a roommate, she would never be able to guess. Not that Jessi wanted to think too much about that. She was just grateful for it happening. There was probably someone in Residential Housing who thought Jessica might be a positive influence on Candi, helping her in her academic work. In reality, it was the other way around. Candi helped Jessi become a hot slut.

But now that Jessi was back in her dorm room, she was at a bit of a loss with what to do with herself. Candi was sitting at her desk, hunched over a textbook. Her tongue stuck out from between her lips ever so slightly, her face screwed up in concentration. Jessi did not know what her roommate was studying, nor did she care, but she felt sorry for her new friend.

"Let's go do something." Jessi's comment came out as a petulant whine. She was bored and still amped up from her experience with Professor Wright. After the weekend she had, Jessi was not quite ready to go back out on the prowl for sex, but she was not that far away from that point either. She had already tried counting the number of men she had been with over the weekend, but she had lost count. Last night's orgy had made it impossible to keep track. She could not even track how many cocks she had sucked.

"Jessi," Candi said, turning to look her roommate in the eye. "I know you're itching to do something, but since I don't have a relationship with a professor like you do, I actually have to study. Why don't you watch a movie or something? That should keep you occupied for a while. Once I'm done with my homework, we can do something together."

Jessi brightened at Candi's idea. A movie was just the ticket of how to spend her time. She pulled out her laptop and laid back on her bed. Admittedly, her laptop had not gotten a lot of use since returning to school. Then again, with her phone, her laptop was less needed. She had it to write papers and perform research on. But with Professor Wright making all of that obsolete, her laptop was now little more than a media hub, mostly to watch movies.

However, Jessi was quickly flummoxed by what she wanted to watch. She had access to streaming accounts, but she could not think of anything worth watching. She had half a mind to ask Candi what she would watch, not knowing what movies were popular at the moment. Movies had never been something Jessi was especially interested in before. She never had time to go to the theater to see a movie. Now that she had friends, she was sure that would change, but she still had little idea what to watch.

Jessi started clicking around, but nothing jumped out at her. That was until an ad started playing on one of the websites she visited. It was for a sex game. Not that Jessi clicked on the ad. She was certain it would give her computer a virus. She might be a horny slut now, but she was no dummy when it came to her computer. She knew not to click on ads like that.

However, that gave Jessi an idea. She was vaguely aware that sex computer games existed, although she had no idea how sophisticated they were. There was no way she was going to play a game like that, but she could certainly enjoy watching someone else play. It would be like watching porn, but different.

It took a few minutes, but Jessi eventually managed to find a streaming site that allowed adult content like that. And before she knew it, she was watching someone play a sex game on their computer. It came with realistic voice acting too, making it all the better.

Candi glanced over her shoulder to see Jessi watching what clearly sounded like porn. She smiled a little, enjoying how far her roommate had managed to come in such a short amount of time. She was actually shocked at how quickly Jessi took to all of this. Candi was vaguely aware of Jessi's past as Jessica. She knew no details, but she could sense the kind of woman Jessi had been before. It said something that Jessi had made such strides in such a short time, because it meant Jessi was serious about this new life.

However, there was no way Candi could study with Jessi watching porn in the room like that. At least not without Jessi wearing headphones.

"Headphones," Candi called out. "I need to concentrate."

"Oh, good idea. Sorry about the noise."

Jessi was well meaning in her apology. She had no intention of upsetting or distracting her roommate. Yes, Jessi would have preferred that they do something together, but that was not to be for now. She quickly grabbed a pair of earbuds and put them in her ears, silencing the sound from the game she watched.

However, that was not the end of the distractions for Candi. At first it went well. Jessi watched her computer while Candi studied. In most other cases, Candi would have gone to the library to study. It was supposed to be a quiet place. But Candi knew she would run into men she could not turn down. Plus, she had a reputation as a bit of a bimbo to uphold. If guys saw her studying in public, she would lose her bimbo credentials.

But none of that was on her mind at the moment. Instead,

it was the soft moans now coming from Jessi as she watched her game. Candi was sure her roommate did not even realize that she was slowly rubbing herself as she watched her laptop. Not wearing panties meant her pussy was more accessible. Most of the time that was not an issue. It could even be considered a good thing when sex was at the forefront of the mind, but in this case, it posed a problem for Candi.

She tried to ignore Jessi's moans. She even put on headphones of her own, the noise canceling variety, attempting to block out Jessi with music. But then Jessi took it up a notch, getting louder and breaking through the noise canceling abilities of the headphones.

"Take it you dirty girl," Jessi moaned, her voice rising in volume as she grew more desperate to cum. "Take that fat cock up your ass."

Jessi went on like that for several minutes, egging on the fake people having sex on her screen. And finally Candi snapped.

"Jessi, I can't take it anymore. Go take a shower or something to cool off. You're killing me over here with your moaning."

Jessi sat up and looked over at her friend. She had been completely unaware that she had been making any noise at all. But she certainly was not going to argue with Candi. If she was moaning, then she believed her friend.

"Sorry," Jessi said, but she did not appear embarrassed by Candi catching her masturbating to the images on her laptop. She was past embarrassment, for the most part. When it came to sex, Jessi was becoming more and more proud of her actions. Sure, men liked to have sex with women, but she was a hot slut who could get any man she wanted. That was something to take pride in.

Of course, that kind of sexualized life required a high libido, which she was now dealing with. Candi was probably right though. After the weekend she had, a shower to cool off seemed like just the ticket. Besides, she was still wearing her schoolgirl outfit and that needed to change.

Jessi turned off her laptop and stripped out of her outfit. That was not particularly difficult, considering how little there was to the outfit, but it was necessary. She was going to need to do some laundry soon too. But a shower was in order first. Jessi wrapped a towel around her body and headed out of the room, not caring if anyone saw her barely covered in a towel. Actually, she kind of hoped a hot guy would come through and rip the towel off her and then fuck her, but that was partly because she was still turned on.

Jessi had to admit, the shower felt good. The hot water streaming over her sensitive skin did wonders for her, making her feel much better. Not that it helped to squelch the fire that her earlier ministrations had lit inside of her. And not caring if anyone overheard her, Jessi went right back to playing with herself, one hand playing with her small breasts and the other circling her clit.

When she added fingers to the mix, pushing them up into her pussy, imagining they were a cock penetrating her hungry pussy, she started to moan. Jessi was past the point of caring if someone heard her. She was not even paying attention to possible noises. All she cared about was the pleasure.

"Oh fuck," Jessi nearly screamed as she finally came. Her body shuddered with orgasmic pleasure as her vision momentarily turned white. Her whole body hummed with erotic sensations as the hot water continued to pound against her skin.

When Jessi's sight returned to her, she was leaning against the shower stall wall, her legs barely able to keep her standing. And it was only then that she heard giggling coming from a nearby stall. Someone had heard her and they thought it was funny. Maybe it was funny. Jessi was certainly smiling, although not because she thought orgasming in the shower was funny. She just felt too good to care.

Stepping out to grab her towel, Jessi was not particularly concerned about her being seen in the nude. She was proud of her body, even if there were aspects of it that could be better. Looking down at herself as she rubbed the towel through her hair, Jessi was more certain than ever that her breasts were too small. Candi was so much bigger. So were the models in the game she had watched. All of them sported much larger and rounder breasts.

And then there were Jessi's lips. Compared to the game models, her lips were thin and far too plain looking. Even Candi and Amy had plumper lips. But Jessi was doing well with what she had. She had no doubts about that. But the question cropped up in her mind of what it would take for Cole to finally fuck her. She knew that was her goal, although she was not entirely sure what else she wanted from him.

The idea of becoming Cole's girlfriend was strong. However, she had no idea all the steps she would have to take to reach that point. And once she did, would she be able to say no to all of that cock. Jessi had never been boy crazy before, but now she certainly was. The only difference was she came at it from a different perspective than most other people. Being a late bloomer had taught her that there was a certain power in being a hot slut. And that was a power she enjoyed. Could she give that up for Cole? Jessi would have to think about that.

But then another smile broke out across Jessi's face as she realized she was going to get to see Cole in the morning. She could not wait to turn herself into putty for his hands and his lips and anything else he wanted to do with her. She might be a hot slut, but she only really had eyes for one man. And someday he would tell her what he desired from her so that they could be together for real.

MORE FAKE IT UNTIL YOU MAKE IT

If you enjoyed this first season of Fake It Until You Make It, be sure to check out the continuing saga of Jessi as she transforms herself into a bimbo as she navigates college life trying to be a popular girl. The latest episodes (chapters) are available every Friday on the Kindle Vella platform. Updates about the story can be found on Tumblr (https://authorsadi ethatcher.tumblr.com/tagged/story) Each season of the story will eventually be published in ebook and paperback formats when ready.

ABOUT THE AUTHOR

Sadie Thatcher is a longtime author of erotic fiction, especially related to transformations and bimbofication. She likes to say "I have thrown off the shackles of my conservative upbringing and now write erotic stories."

She maintains a special blog devoted to her writings, including a behind the scenes look at her writing process, and bimbos in general, as well as highlights works by other authors. They can be found at:

https://authorsadiethatcher.tumblr.com

twitter.com/Sadie_Thatcher

Bimbo Dome

Acting the Part

Subliminal Society

Inheritance

Company Morale

His Bimbo Girlfriend

The Bimbo Room

The Bimbos of Blossom

Dr. Jekyll and Missy Hyde

Second Chance

From M&As To T&A

Trading Places

The Bimbo Nutcracker Suite

Milked and Herded

Fitting In

Clowning Around

Transformative Ink

Choices

Rival Competition

Alien Womanhood

Invasion

The Princess and the Bimbo

Bimbo Labyrinth

The Legend of the Werebimbo

Power and Corruption

The Simulation

The Curse of Playing Bimbo Tag

The Curse of Playing Bimbo Tag: Jenna or Jenni

The Bimbo Professor: The Curse of Playing Bimbo Tag Book 3

Anything for the Job

Anything for the Job 2

Anything for His Job

The Bimbo in the Mirror

The Bimbo in the Mirror 2

Astrid and the Bimbo Bee

Bella and the Bimbo Bee

Cali and the Bimbo Bee

Desiree and the Bimbo Bee

Ember and the Bimbo Bee

Fiona and the Bimbo Bee

The Intern

The Lawyer

The Hacker

Cause & Effect

Witless Protection

Stealing Sally

Trial and Error

Beta Testing

Exposed

Bimbo for a Weekend

Bimbo for a Week

Bimbo for Life

Fake It Until You Make It Season 1

Simple and Fun Volume 1

Simple and Fun Volume 2

Simple and Fun Volume 3

Simple and Fun Volume 4

Simple and Fun Volume 5

Simple and Fun Volume 6

Bimbo Halloween

Bimbo Christmas

Bimbo Technology

Dorm Room Bimbo

Carissa's Magic Pen

Spirit Walk

Muscle Memory

The Case of the Bimbo Wife

Changes

Changes 2

New Year New You

The Bimbo Dream

The Wedding Gift

The Cure

Backfire

Bim & Bo Yoga

Wishing for Each Other

Bimbo Roots

A Bimbo at Oktoberfest

The Lost Bet

The Fountain

Bimbo Ghost

Sugar and Spice and Everything Nice

Basic Bimbo

A Helping Hand

Bimbos in Space

Christmas Train to Bimboton

Letters to Bimbo Claus

Gone Fishing

The Bimbo Behind the Mask

Rival Wishes

What's in a Name?

Playing the Game

Friendly Wishes

My Chemical Bimbo

To Be Young Again

Something Bimbo Calls Him Home

Wishing for Him

The Author Gets Bimbofied

Bigfoot and the Bimbo

Bimbo Zero

Going Native

Thanks for Giving

Working for Bimbo Claus

The Spirit of Bimbo Christmas

The Bimbo Sweater

What Really Happened to D.B. Cooper

Starting Over

Milk and Bliss

The Fighter

The Help

Body Swap Rings: Happy Anniversary

Body Swap Rings 2: Wedding Night

The Bimbo Experience

The Bimbo Experience 2

The Bimbo Experience 3some

The 4th Bimbo Experience

Bimbo Genes

Bimbo Genes II: The Virus

The Bimbo Genes III: The Epidemic

Bimbo Juice: Blue Raspberry

Bimbo Juice: Grape

Bimbo Juice: Mango

Bimbo Juice: Pineapple

Bimbo Juice: Red Apple

Bimbo Juice: Veggie

Bimbo Juice Gone Wild: The Muse

Bimbo Juice Gone Wild: Street Racer

Bimbo Juice Gone Wild: Score

Bimbos of the Traveling Earrings: Book 1

Bimbos of the Traveling Earrings: Book 2

Bimbos of the Traveling Earrings: Book 3

Bimbos of the Traveling Earrings: Book 4

Bimbo Party: Kennedy

Bimbo Party: Esme

Bimbo Party: Ariana

Bimbo Party: Tara

Workout Buddies

Wishful Thinking

Wanting More

Bimbo Harem: Annabelle

Bimbo Harem: Josie

Bimbo Harem: Nikki

Bimbo Harem: Tiana

Giggle Dust

Giggle Dust 2.0

Giggle Dust 3.0

Giggle Dust 4.0

Bimbo Takeover: The First Step

Bimbo Takeover: Teammates

Bimbo Takeover: Going to the Top

Bimbo Takeover: Revenge of the Bimbos

Thanks for the Mammaries

A New Beginning

Copying Kat

Spreading the Love

Discovering Eden

Building Eden

Spring In Eden

Saving Eden

The Perfect Girlfriend

The Perfect Engagement

The Perfect Wife

The Perfect Woman

Be Hot, Not Smart

No Thoughts for Thots

Be Art, Not Smart

The Cream of the Crop

A New Kind of Passion